"Why didn't you let us know that you were still alive?"

Mike shot her a penetrating look. "I didn't get back to the States until three years after David's death, and I was in and out of hospitals for about a year. When I was well enough I called, but a baby-sitter answered and said you were out with your fiancé." He sounded faintly accusing. "Obviously you'd recovered."

"David had been dead four years, and we'd been happy together. I wanted that happiness again."

"*Are* you happy again?"

"I didn't remarry, if that's what you mean."

Something flickered across his face, and Carolyn wondered what he would say if she told him that for some reason, because he was here, her life was complete for the first time since she'd lost David.

DORIS RANGEL was a schoolteacher before she "threw caution to the winds, sold my house and moved West . . . well, West Texas, anyway. Believe me," she says, "it is just like those old movies: rugged mountains, harsh deserts, deer and antelope and slow-talking cowboys that really do ride horses." She now lives on five acres in the Davis Mountains and has plans to open a second-hand bookstore. With three children she laments the lack of time for hobbies. However, she is a prodigious reader and loves to garden. Her goal in life is to ride in a hot-air balloon over the Serengeti at dawn the year after she takes a Smithsonian Institute tour of Tibet by way of mainland China.

DORIS RANGEL

legacy

Harlequin Books

TORONTO • NEW YORK • LONDON
AMSTERDAM • PARIS • SYDNEY • HAMBURG
STOCKHOLM • ATHENS • TOKYO • MILAN

Harlequin Presents first edition April 1986
ISBN 0-373-10878-8

Original hardcover edition published in 1985
by Mills & Boon Limited

Printed in U.S.A.

CHAPTER ONE

CAROLYN sighed and put down her book. She had read the same page three times in the course of the last twenty minutes and it still was incomprehensible. It was her own fault, really. She just couldn't seem to concentrate. The sound of the rain beating against the cabin windows, ordinarily so soothing, was filling her with a mental restlessness that would not allow her to follow the intricacies of the Eastern Philosophy she was trying to study. Her mind seemed to jump from one irrelevancy to another, any innocent phrase setting it off in a new tangent. It was best to give it up for a while and begin preparing the stew she and Michael would be having later that evening. It was a little early, she supposed, but she needed to be busy and venison stew was one of those meals that tasted better the longer it cooked.

Michael, lying on his stomach in front of the fire and playing with a pocket video game, obviously heard the sigh and gave her an impish grin. 'What's the matter, Mom? Too hard for you?' She was a good student and Michael was quite proud of his mother's good grades but that didn't stop him from teasing at every opportunity.

'Show your old mother some respect, son, or I'll show you I've been holding out in our next chess game,' she grinned back at him, giving his prone body a gentle dig with her toe as she passed him on her way to the kitchen. They both knew it was an empty threat and she answered his 'Ha!' with a laugh of her own. Her son, no dummy himself she proudly acknowledged, could beat her hands down at that game of strategy with his mind on something else.

Still smiling, she walked over to the kitchen area to begin preparations for their evening meal. She readied the camp stove and then began cubing and seasoning the deer meat that would be the foundation of the stew. As she worked she hummed an old, sentimental dance tune.

Carolyn loved this cabin. It was a part of her. She and David had built it themselves in the first year of their marriage. The land it sat on, high in the Rocky Mountains, had been a joint wedding gift from their respective parents and she and David had honeymooned here. She smiled at the memory.

What a glorious six days it had been! At the crucial time seven days had been all the leave that David had been allowed and they had spent as much of it as possible on 'their' mountain. Not wasting any of it, they had alternately filled the time with making love and making plans for the cabin they would build here. In those few days they had paced out its dimensions, marked the trees they would have to cut for its construction, and gathered the stones from the stream that would go into the building of the fireplace.

It had only two rooms—a kitchen-living area and a bedroom, each in generous proportions. It was furnished with a combination of furniture that had been made 'on the spot' by David and that which had been dismantled, packed by horseback up the mountain, and then reassembled. There was no electricity but there was running water if one used the old-fashioned pump handle at the sink. There was even an indoor toilet for which David had devised the plumbing and of which he had been immensely proud.

The cabin was plain to the extreme, she supposed, looking around with loving eyes. Yet she and David had poured their laughter and love and dreams into the creation of it—into every swing of the axe and blow of the hammer, into every drop of sweat and even into the swear words. Here had centred their hopes for the future.

They would live here when David's stint in the military was over and he would write his novel. He had had a few articles and short stories published but he had a novel running around in his head, he had said, that was begging for release. She was going to settle to the equally serious business of starting a family and, she had teased him, two rooms wouldn't be enough for long. He had answered with the not-quite-accurate fact that they had the whole mountain on which to enlarge the cabin so she could do her worse—or best! They had joked and laughed and loved and dreamed.

When David had received his Southeast Asian assignment they had come here, of course, on his last leave before being shipped out. He had assured her he was being sent in an advisory capacity only, that there would be no fighting. But she, with the recent horrors of Viet-Nam in her memory, had been afraid. To pledge their faith in each other and in the future they had deliberately taken no precautions and Michael had been conceived, much to their mutual delight. 'I'll add another room as soon as I get home,' David had written when Carolyn had notified him of the doctor's confirmation of what she had known as she lay in David's arms.

The room was never added. The laughter and the love are still here for Michael and me, Carolyn thought, but the dreams died with David in that far-off land. Yet the cabin still provided her with a place to renew her spirit and helped Michael to come in some measure of contact with the father he had never known.

Carolyn gave herself a mental shake and noted with surprise how much her hands had accomplished towards the stew as her mind had been elsewhere. As she added water, salt, pepper, and a bayleaf to the braised meat she happened to glance out the window and saw with surprise that while she had been daydreaming, the weather had turned nasty, the rain now icy and mixed with snow. She saw that the thermometer hanging outside the window showed a drop of several degrees below freezing. The wind had also increased and was wailing around the corners of the cabin.

So that's the reason for the restlessness, she thought, her tension and lack of concentration clicking into place. All her life she had been sensitive to weather changes and it was a source of great amusement to her son, as it had been to his father before him. This similarity in their sense of humour filled her with a warm joy for she felt that this was but another gift from his father to the son he would never see.

'Michael,' she said now, 'turn on the radio and see if you can find a weather forecast.'

'Why?' he teased. 'Are we going to have an Easter blizzard?'

'I think so,' she answered him seriously, 'and the weather outside seems to confirm it.' His grin died as he immediately went to get the portable radio they always kept with fresh batteries in case of emergencies. His mother's gift made him laugh, but he believed in it implicitly. Sitting down at the table, he turned the radio at several angles, going up and down the dial, but could get nothing but disjointed phrases and static.

'If I'm right, and I think I am,' she said regretfully,

coming to stand beside him as he manipulated the radio, 'we are going to have to stay indoors for the next few days. I'm sorry, honey,' and she gave his shoulders a hug, marvelling that she could still do so. She knew that Michael, at ten, would still accept these casual caresses as a part of their relationship. Soon, however, he would want to start loosening the apron strings and spontaneous hugs would become an embarrassment to him. Her little boy was growing up so fast.

'I can use the time to improve your chess game,' he said smugly, wrinkling his nose at her.

She laughed. 'You can only try. In the meantime, you had better check the horses and make sure they have enough feed to last a while since it may be late tomorrow before we can get back to the stable. Also, I think you had better run a line from our door to the one on the stable. I have a feeling we may need it before this is over.'

'And we know those feelings, don't we?' he grinned.

'Scoot now,' she ordered. 'And, Michael,' as he stood at the door bundled in his outdoor things, 'perhaps you had better bring in some wood, just in case. In fact, I'd better help you.'

'Do you think it will be that bad? We already have a lot in.'

'Yes, I think it will be that bad, but in any case, it's better to be on the safe side.'

She went to put on her own outdoor wear, tugging on her boots, pulling an extra-heavy knit pullover sweater over her head, then shrugging on a ski jacket. Last of all, she pushed her shining, shoulder length, 'just plain brown' hair into a crimson knitted cap. This was done quickly, for she had looked through the window at the thermometer and saw that the temperature was dropping almost as she watched.

Outdoors, the wind was so strong she had trouble

shutting the cabin door. She thought to herself that it was a good thing she hadn't waited longer. With the blowing rain and snow she could barely see the forest across the clearing. Fighting her way to the woodpile, she filled her arms with as much wood as she could carry and staggered back towards the cabin.

The weather was setting in to be really bad, but Carolyn wasn't worried. She and Michael had waited out too many blizzards on this mountain to cause her any sense of panic. The cabin was snug and cosy, they had plenty of food and supplies, and neither of them had to be back to school for another three weeks. They had only arrived yesterday and there was plenty of time for the mountain to work its peaceful magic. Carolyn was teaching on an assistantship at the university where she was taking her Doctorate Degree and she was mentally tired. Lazing in front of a crackling fire as a blizzard howled outside was not unappealing.

As she neared the door she met Michael coming from the stable. He took some of the wood from her arms and opened the cabin door for her. Inside they deposited their load near the wood bin and turned to go back for more. Before doing so, however, Carolyn stopped to light the lantern. The interior of the cabin was already becoming gloomy. As she was doing this, Michael asked diffidently, 'Mom, when you were outside, did you . . . *hear* anything?'

'Only the wind,' she answered. 'Why?'

'When I was going to the stable I thought I heard the whinny of a horse. The sound didn't seem to come from the direction of our stable.'

'Maybe it was a trick of the wind shifting the sound around,' she reasoned. 'No one ever comes as high as this even in good weather.'

'Yeah, I guess that was it.' He shrugged and they

both went out again into the howling, blowing wind and gathering darkness.

The wind seemed to have increased and the blowing snow was already drifting over the wood pile. They both filled their arms with as much wood as they could carry and turned to go back. Carolyn was glad she had taken the time to light the lantern since now it acted as a beacon to the warm cabin. As they neared the door the wind seemed to take a short respite and in the comparative silence both of them were startled to hear the sound of a walking horse. The eeriness of the situation caused the skin at the back of Carolyn's neck to prickle and she elbowed Michael's arms to urge him up the step to the cabin. It seemed as if the horse was coming nearer and they could hear an additional sound that Carolyn could not identify. She dropped her wood by the cabin door, as did Michael, and turned to peer through the white ghostly gloom but could see nothing. The wind had picked up again and she could hear only its rising howl.

She unlatched the door and the wind immediately tore it from her hands to slam against the inside wall. Michael was at her heels and it took both of them to close it again. They stood several minutes beside the closed door staring wide-eyed at each other, straining to hear the sounds of someone's arrival but could hear nothing save the eerie moaning of the wind. 'Could be a horse that has strayed from one of the ranches and is looking for shelter,' Carolyn said finally. She hated the little snake of fear that was twisting inside of her and with sudden resolve she went to the nail where an extra coil of rope was hung and took it down. Tying one end around her waist, she grinned at her son. 'I'll be a nervous wreck until I know what's out there. Hang onto this loose end in case I need to have help in

finding my way back. If I give two hard tugs like this,'
and she demonstrated, 'that means I need you. Tie your
end of the rope to the door handle and follow it to me.
Got it?'

'Ah, Mom! Can't I come with you?'

'No,' she said firmly. 'I need you here. Okay?'

'Okay,' he answered regretfully, 'but be careful!'

'I'm always careful,' she grinned. 'Now I'm depending
on you to hold this rope good and tight. I don't want to
give a jerk and pull it right out of your hands!'

'I've got it tight,' he assured her and she opened the
door to head once more into the blowing swirling
whiteness. When she was about ten feet from the cabin
she again heard a horse slowly walking, accompanied
by that other ghostly sound. The sound stopped as the
horse again stopped. She turned towards where she
thought the sound was coming from and struggled on
through the buffeting, freezing wind.

'Halloo!' she called. 'Who's there?' There was no
answer but the sound of the horse once more coming
closer with its accompanying drag. Drag? That's what
the sound was! She peered through the gloom and
through a break in the snow flurries, saw a riderless
horse only a few yards ahead of her. 'Steady, boy,
steady,' she called as the horse shied at her approach
but it quietened as she neared him. 'The cavalry has
arrived,' she assured him in a calm voice, 'and we'll
soon have you warm and fed. But where is your rider?'
when she was near enough to see that the horse wore a
saddle.

Because of the blowing snow she was at the animal's
side before the question answered itself. The rider was
lying on his back in the snow, his body powdered with
it, and one large boot was caught in the stirrup. Here
was the reason for the dragging noise and why the

horse had walked so slowly and had stopped so often. The rider was unconscious or dead, Carolyn couldn't tell which.

Her heart pounding, she fumbled until she had his boot unhooked from the stirrup. Then she crouched down to brush the snow from his face. She was glad to see the enveloping hood of his parka had given his face some protection. As she leaned over to push the edges aside she found herself looking into a pair of deep brown eyes sunken in a face grey with cold and something else. The eyes, holding her own mesmerized, examined her face minutely and then blinked once slowly. Carolyn caught her breath. She could swear there was a smile in their velvet depths. Before she could be sure, the lashes fanned slowly down again and this time remained closed as the man once more lapsed into unconsciousness. Or was he dead? His face had relaxed into lines of contentment associated with death.

Carolyn, released to breathe again, scanned the face trying to place someone she might know. She had the oddest feeling this man had recognised her, but she knew that she had never seen him before. He had an arresting, memorable face. Besides those overpowering eyes, he had a nose that had either been quite badly broken, or had been broken more than once—like that of a prize fighter. And that mouth! It was as gentle as sensitive as a girl's. But now it twisted as the face contorted and the man gave a soft moan. Well, I know he's not dead, Carolyn thought, and a deep sense of relief flooded through her. She knew that he soon would be if she didn't quickly get him back to the cabin.

How? He was a big man, apparently quite tall and with a massive build. His outdoor clothing added to his bulk, of course, but he looked enormous! She thought frantically. There was no way she could get him to the cabin by herself and doubted that even with Michael to help they could drag him that far. They couldn't get him back on the horse and it would take too long to get the gear together to rig a travois that would allow the horse to drag him Indian style. But maybe she could move him like she sometimes moved heavy furniture at the apartment, when it had no wheels and was too heavy to slide. She would work a large floor rug under whatever it was she wanted to move and then pull the floor rug. The heavy furniture would then slide quite easily over the floor. It was worth a try and certainly no other solution presented itself.

She grasped the horse's reins with one hand so that it wouldn't bolt and then gave a piercing whistle for Michael, at the same time giving the rope a sharp yank. 'Michael, can you hear me?' she shouted. Fortunately, the wind was blowing in the same direction she was shouting and helped to sweep her words towards their destination. The rope was yanked back as she heard a muffled answering shout. 'Bring a blanket ... our strongest blanket!' she yelled as loudly as she could in the blowing wind, and gave two strong jerks on the rope for good measure.

Two jerks were returned, showing, she hoped, that Michael had understood. It seemed forever, but she knew it was only a few minutes later, that she saw him following the rope to her through the blowing snow. By now, visibility was down to just a few feet. The blanket was one she had hung on the cabin wall to use as a wall hanging. It was an Indian blanket, hand-woven and of excellent quality, and there wasn't a stronger piece of cloth in the cabin. Carolyn had treated herself to its beauty in a moment of weak extravagance a few summers ago. Now she blessed it, at the same time regretting the damage that was bound to occur.

Michael took one look at the situation and asked no questions. Helping her to unfold the blanket and finding rocks under the snow to hold it down in the wind, he worked with the same efficiency and economy of movement as she.

It took both of them to get the unconscious rider on to the blanket. They went by halves, first getting the head and upper torso on and then picking up his legs from the feet and lining him up. Carolyn and Michael were both panting, for the man was heavy and the wind seemed to pull the breath from their bodies. Each grabbed a corner of the blanket and began pulling towards the cabin, using the rope to guide them. They could see nothing now but swirling snow and would have become easily disoriented without its guidance. It was hard, heavy work. The man's inert weight rocked back and forth and had a tendency to slide towards the bottom of the blanket. His legs had been too long to fit completely and his boots dragged in the snow, pulling his body downward. They had to stop often and grab him under the arms to hitch him back up.

They pulled what surely was well over fiften stone of dead weight and both she and Michael were gasping for breath and sweating. That, too, was dangerous with the temperature near the zero mark and the wind chill far below that. Carolyn knew that she and Michael needed to get to the cabin as desperately as the injured man they were pulling. There was no telling what this treatment was doing to any injuries he might have, Carolyn thought tiredly, but she could think of no alternative. The horse, mercifully, followed them on its own.

At last they came within sight of the cabin's

welcoming light. The glowing window filled them with renewed energy as they pulled the last few feet to the cabin door.

Michael opened the door which the wind promptly jerked out of his hands, and then turned to help her get the injured man inside. Here, however, seemed to be a major block, for try as they might, they could not get the man over the step and across the threshold.

They pulled and tugged to no avail, twisting and turning at every possible angle, so desperately intent on their task that they paid little attention to their burden. They were tugging so hard on the blanket that when the man on it stood up—way up—they both tumbled into the snow.

'Okay, let's get inside,' he said in a voice that sounded like it was coming from a cavern. Under their startled gaze he picked up the blanket, folded it neatly, and as Carolyn and Michael slowly rose to their feet and stood gaping, placed a large hand at the small of each of their backs and propelled them through the door, closing it easily behind them.

'Have the men taken care of,' he rapped out, looking around the cabin.

Carolyn looked at Michael, who looked back at her with equal consternation. Were there more people out there? They had heard nothing but the one horse, but of course they had been unable to see a thing and the howling of the wind would have drowned out more distant sounds.

'How many others are there?' Carolyn asked worriedly. She was afraid that if this man had become separated from his party they might have missed her cabin completely in the storm.

'Twelve,' he snapped. 'Does losing eight men go beyond your arithmetic? Post a sentry. Tell them they can take a short break but stay under cover. They can smoke, but for God's sake, tell them to hold down the noise. We can't afford more casualties. Ke Chong is still another day's march and the enemy is covering every foot of it.'

Again Carolyn and Michael looked at each other and Carolyn felt a sinking sensation in the pit of her stomach. What had she done? This man was mad. And the size of him! He was at least six to eight inches over six feet. David had been six feet tall and this man would have towered over him. What if he took it into his head to murder them both, imagining them to be the enemy? You read about such things happening all the time in the papers. And it was her own fault. She had literally dragged him to the cabin! Michael, too, was looking frightened.

At that moment the man raised a long arm and Carolyn and Michael visibly jumped. But he was only reaching up to push back the hood of the parka and then to rub his eyes and face wearily with a still gloved hand. 'God, I'm tired!' he muttered and seemed to sway on his feet.

As his hand fell to his side, Carolyn looked at his face clearly and then knew without a doubt that her fears were groundless. His flushed face and overly bright eyes, combined with what she had seen in the snow made her suddenly realise that this man was extremely ill and was using every internal resource just to stand. She doubted that he had the strength to murder anyone. 'It's all right, Mike,' she assured her son, relief colouring her voice. To the man she said, 'We'll take care of everything. Now you need to rest,' and she went towards him to lead him to the bedroom where he could lie down. She was worried that he would collapse any moment for he looked at the end of his tether. The problem was that wherever he fell would be where he would have to stay.

Before she could touch him, however, he grabbed her shoulder and bit out, 'Who do you think you're talking to, soldier? You call me Sergeant and don't you forget it! Privates don't first name their sergeants even in the middle of a war.' He gave her shoulder a sharp shake for emphasis that made her teeth rattle. Carolyn knew she would have a bruise later where the fingers had gripped, but the hold was immediately slackened as the man again swayed slightly. 'So tired,' he mumbled again and now seemed to use his grip on her shoulder to steady himself.

'All right, sergeant, anything you say,' Carolyn soothed. 'Why don't you come lie down for awhile and rest,' and she used his hold on her shoulder to lead him towards the bedroom. 'We'll take care of everything,' she said again, motioning Michael to get on the other side of him. Michael only came up to his belt buckle but Carolyn thought she might need all the help she could get before they reached the bed.

Indeed, by the time they were to the bedroom he was leaning heavily on her and, as she finally sat him on the side of the big brass bed (what a trick that had been to get up the mountain!), Carolyn felt she could have gone no further. She had barely been able to support him as they staggered the last few feet. She stood panting, trying to catch her breath. There was much to do and quickly. She had felt the fever in him even through his heavy jacket.

He had not as yet passed out, and Carolyn prayed that he would not until she removed his jacket and shirt. The back of his jacket was sodden where he had lain in the snow. He was occasionally muttering softly now in broken, disjointed sentences and it was clear that he was oblivious to his surroundings. His eyes were vacant and unfocused, his face full of hectic colour. Carolyn verified a high fever with a hand to his forehead. She knew by touch that his temperature was far over the danger mark.

Michael, standing beside her, still looked frightened for he had never been around anyone who acted like this and who handled his mother so roughly. Carolyn realised she hadn't explained to him what was wrong and said quietly, 'He has a very high fever, honey, and is very sick. That is what is making him act strange. He just doesn't know who we are and thinks we're in the army.'

She smiled and Michael's bewildered face cleared. If his mom could smile things weren't too bad and sickness was something he understood. His mother was very good at taking care of sick people. She always knew what to do when he wasn't feeling well. The situation caught his interest now that the element of danger to his parent was past.

'Michael, I am going to need your help,' she was saying briskly. 'We have to take care of this man's horse. It is probably still standing beside the door and will freeze it he's not sheltered and fed. Do you think you can put him in the stable?'

'Sure, Mom! I'm on my way,' he answered quickly and made to go to the door.

'Be careful,' she stopped him. 'You saw how blinding storms like this can be. We were almost on top of the cabin before we could see the light ... and it's getting worse, not better. Follow the line you ran earlier to the stable. Give the horse a good rubdown and feed him. Then follow the rope back. In fact, do as I did earlier and tie a rope around yourself and the door handle just to be extra safe. I'm going to worry the entire time

you're gone, so humour an old lady and be super
careful, okay?'

'Okay, Mom,' and he was out the door.

When he was gone, Carolyn quickly shrugged off her
outdoor things. The man sat docilely on the side of the
bed, quiet now but looking as if it was taking every
effort for him to sit without falling over, much as if he
had too much to drink. 'It's all right, sergeant,' she said
softly. 'Just as soon as we get you out of these damp
things you can lie down,' and she pulled off each of his
gloves. As she did so, she saw that around each of his
wrists was a network of scar tissue. Almost like obscene
bracelets, the scars stood out whitely against the tan of
his arms and hands. She looked into the man's face,
silently questioning, but of course there was nothing
there to answer.

She went on talking soft nonsense, letting the sound
of her voice flow over him as she unzipped his parka
and slipped his arms out of the sleeves. He didn't
answer and he didn't help her, but his head was tilted
slightly as if he listened intently to every word.

The back of his red plaid shirt was also damp and
she pulled his shirt tail from his pants and quickly
began undoing the buttons. Her fingers shook slightly
as she fumbled with the fastenings and she gave a
whispered, 'Damn!' at her own clumsiness. Some slight
movement caused her to look up and she caught her
breath. Again, she had the strangest feeling that way
down deep inside himself the man was smiling—but his
mouth held no trace of a quirk and not a muscle in his
face moved. She looked into his eyes but they, too, had
that slightly unfocused look.

'Now I'm imagining things,' she muttered. 'Look,
Sarge,' knowing he didn't really hear her, 'I'm not used
to undressing strange men, or any men for that matter,'

and she went back to her task, this time without
trembling. As she pulled his arms from each sleeve she
continued to talk to herself. Undressing a man in a
semi-stupor was nerve wracking, at best, and the sound
of her own voice calmed her somewhat. 'The last time I
undressed a man was the last time David and I made
love,' she now said softly. Her face took on a soft glow
with the thought. 'That was when Michael was
conceived.'

The man moaned softly and she quickly pulled off
the remainder of the shirt. He looked as if he were in
pain and Carolyn knew she would have to check for
injuries that might have been sustained when he fell and
was dragged by the horse.

He wore a white, long sleeved, thermal undershirt
under his outer shirt that was standard wear for man or
woman travelling on horseback in the high valleys of
the Rockies in early spring. There were no bloodstains
on its whiteness but she would have to take it off to
examine him more thoroughly and it would have to
come over his head. To cut it up in order to get it off
more easily would only be a last resort. If he left this
mountain again he would need its protection. Carolyn's
jaw clenched at the thought of that 'if'.

Standing between his legs in front of him where he
sat on the edge of the bed, she gently eased his
shoulders towards her so that she could examine his
head for any signs of injury. But when she let go of his
shoulders to do this his head continued to fall forward
and his forehead gently came to rest at the top of her
breasts. She found herself supporting the weight of his
upper torso, the heat from his face seeming to burn into
her breasts. She stood shocked for a moment, her hands
clenched at her side, at the very intimacy of their
position. There swept over her the almost overwhelming

desire to put her arms around him and hold him tightly. She swallowed convulsively and, taking him by the shoulders, tried to straighten him up once more, but he was completely inert. Having at last reached the end of his remarkable endurance, he had passed out.

'Oh, Sarge, you make things so difficult,' she whispered resignedly. With no alternative, she allowed his head to rest against her, turning his face to the side so that his cheek was pillowed in the softness of her breasts, ignoring how right the feel of it there was to her. Gently she ran her fingers through his tight, rusty-brown curls but she could find no cuts or bumps. Then she set about the business of removing his undershirt.

She did it with him leaning against her in much the same way that she had removed Michael's pullovers when he was a baby and able to sit up but not alone. It was more difficult, of course, due to the man's size but using her body as a prop she managed at last to pull the shirt over his head without jostling him too much.

It was then she found the second network of scars, this time encircling the base of his neck. These were not as pronounced as those on his wrists and seemed to have faded somewhat with time. The pictures the scars conjured were terrible but there was no time for speculation. The room was warm but the man was burning with fever and needed to be covered as quickly as possible.

She ran her fingers over his back and ribs and could feel her cheeks flushing and a warm weakness beginning in the pit of her stomach. It had been years since she had touched a man so intimately. She found no injuries.

Carolyn tried to keep her mind on the immediacy of the situation as, holding him balanced against her with one arm, his face still pressed into her breasts, she used the other to pull back the covers from the bed.

Lowering him gently sideways until his head was on the pillow, she then swung his legs up, straightening him until he was lying on his back.

She stepped back and for the first time looked her fill at the man who now lay in her bed. He certainly was an enigma. Each feature was a contradiction. Overall, he looked to be in his thirties, but which end of the scale was difficult to determine. His mouth was the most kissable one in a man that she had ever seen, yet she would bet that his nose had been broken in a fight he hadn't lost. And his eyes! She was glad they were closed. They frightened her. She had a feeling that if she looked into them too long she would fall in without resistance and sink into the man's very soul. He had the brawn of a stevedore, and the hands of an artist. The palms were hard and calloused, but the fingers were finely shaped, long and tapering, looking as if they would be equally comfortable holding an eighteenth century Dresden figurine or a sledge hammer.

Unable to help herself, Carolyn reached out and ran a finger along the top of his hand and down the index finger. His nails were cut short and were clean and well manicured. The hand trembled slightly under her touch and she snatched her own away as if burned.

She was suddenly glad there was no time to examine feelings she had thought never to have again. 'You aren't going to get better with me standing here looking at you,' she said aloud and swung a soft blanket over his chest and shoulders before going to the foot of the bed to remove his boots.

CHAPTER TWO

SHE was struggling with the second boot when she heard the cabin door slam with Michael's entry. 'Thank God,' she said aloud sincerely, for Michael had been constantly at the back of her mind.

'Did everything go all right?' she asked as he came into the room bringing with him the cool, fresh scent of the outdoors.

'Sure, no problem,' he answered with all the understatement of a ten year old. 'Need any help?'

'Yes. I'm going to take his jeans off and it will be much easier if you help me,' she said matter-of-factly, undoing the belt buckle. In spite of herself, her fingers trembled with her self-consciousness but she willed her face to show no sign of her feelings. She was glad Michael was here. Between them they succeeded in taking off the man's pants and Carolyn was not surprised that he wore the bottom part of the thermal underwear beneath his jeans. They, too, were standard winter wear. Carolyn looked at them a moment before saying, 'He might need those for warmth later, so we'll leave them on. His socks, too.'

'Sure, Mom, anything you say.' Michael's face was innocent of expression but his eyes held a distinct twinkle. Carolyn gave him what she hoped was a chastening look in spite of her warm cheeks.

They pulled the blankets up over the inert figure and, as Carolyn picked up the discarded clothing from the floor, Michael stood looking at the man on the bed, examining him much as she had done earlier. 'You know, Mom, he looks like an all right guy,' he pronounced finally, in tones that gave his seal of approval. At his words, Carolyn again had the strange feeling that the man was smiling, though his eyes were closed and there was no trace of movement in his face.

She had reached much the same conclusion herself. 'You may be right,' she told her son, 'but if he is going to be really an all right guy, we are going to have to get that fever down as quickly as possible.'

She went to the cabinet where she kept the first-aid supplies but found pitiful armour against whatever was wrong with him. She felt instinctively that he had brought the fever with him to the mountain and because of it, had lost consciousness and fallen from his horse, but she had no idea of the fever's cause. She had found no injuries or signs of outward infection to explain it, so it had to caused by something internal. Perhaps he had a severe case of the flu. But surely he would have known what was wrong with him before starting up the mountain. Whatever it was, cold and exposure had made it worse and she had only aspirin to give him. What he needed were antibiotics. This was one of the few times she regretted being so far from civilisation. The fever thermometer had only confirmed her worst fears.

Michael brought her some water and she poured a little of it into a glass, dropping in as many aspirin as she dared. 'Hold him for me until I get this down him,' she directed and, as Michael held his shoulders, she held the man's head steady with one hand while using the other to hold the liquid to his lips. For all her efforts the mixture dribbled down his chin. She was close to tears in her anxiety and finally said desperately, almost angrily, 'Look, Sarge, we can't do it all. You have to help. Now drink this, damn it!' Michael looked at her in surprise. His mother seldom used profanity but it seemed to work. The man managed to swallow most of the aspirin down.

'Now, honey, one more thing and then you can go fix yourself some stew,' she said to Michael as they laid the man gently back against the pillows. 'I know you're starving,' and she smiled because 'I'm starving' was an often heard chorus. 'Bring the kerosene heater we thought we'd never use. I'm going to bathe him and see if that will bring down his fever. This room will have to be as warm as we can get it.'

With the heater, the room began to fill with added warmth and she sent Michael to the kitchen to get some stew and to relax. 'I won't need you anymore for a while,' she smiled and added seriously, 'I don't know that I would have done without you.'

'I don't know what you would have done, either, Mom,' he grinned cheekily and she gave him an affectionate hug.

Carolyn rubbed the man down with alcohol and when she had used up her small supply, brought a basin of water and some washcloths and began bathing him with the tepid water. Over and over she bathed his face and neck and chest and shoulders and arms and hands, changing the cloths often as she went through the process and then starting all over again, losing track of time, hoping for any sign that it was doing some good, for she didn't know what else to do. She was a teacher, not a nurse, but she knew that this man needed more expert care than she could give. Her own back and shoulders were on fire when she looked up to find Michael by her side. 'I've fixed you some stew, Mom. Go on and eat and I'll stay a while.'

'I won't argue,' she said tiredly. 'I don't believe I'm doing him any good anyway, but I don't dare give him any more aspirin just yet.' She was desperately worried.

When she went into the other room, rubbing her neck tiredly, she found that Michael had indeed left a big bowl of stew on the table in readiness for her and in addition, a fresh pot of coffee sat on the stove. As she ate, she thanked God that out of all the children in the world He had given her Michael. She tacked on a plea for the sick man in her bed.

The coffee was good but she was too worried to linger over it. Pouring a cup to take with her she went back into the bedroom to find Michael doing the same as she had done, washing the still unconscious man's face and arms and torso over and over again. As he washed, he talked. 'You just have to hurry up and get well, Sarge. I want to ask you about your horse. He's a beauty! And I have this great new video game. It's hard, but I'll bet I can beat you at it. I'm good at games, you know. I beat Mom all the time in chess.'

'My, you're full of yourself, aren't you?' she teased him, coming into the room. 'Hmm, but he's looking better,' and he did, the hectic colour having left his face. She took his temperature again and for the first time felt a flicker of hope. 'It is still too high but it's at least a couple of degrees lower than it was.'

She took over from Michael and after that she and the boy alternated, each talking softly to the man as they repeatedly washed him, willing him to get better, praying that the cool water would pull the heat from his body. When Carolyn felt enough time had elapsed, they gave him more of the aspirin and water.

Near midnight, she ordered Mike to bed, overcoming his sleepy protests with the promise to call him if he was needed. The man was better, she assured him. Though he still had a temperature, it was no longer as such a dangerous level. They could both use a little rest and she would nap in the chair by the bed. She walked with Michael into the other room to help him roll out his sleeping bag on the rug in front of the fire, now banked for the night. This had been his bed since he had outgrown his carrycot and he loved it. 'Goodnight,' she whispered when he was curled inside, pushing his hair gently back from his forehead.

' 'Night,' he murmured, already three quarters asleep.

Carolyn was smiling as she went back to the bedroom and approached the bed. The man was lying on his back with his face turned slightly towards the pillow. He looked as if he were finally in a natural sleep and she hoped he was. She put out a hand and brushed the curls off his forehead, much as she had done Michael's. ' 'Night, Sarge,' she said softly. At her whispered words his cheek seemed to nestle more fully into the pillow. The gesture filled her with unexpected tenderness and, afraid of her feelings, she moved quickly away from the bed.

She turned the lantern down so that it emitted only a soft glow and then checked the floor heater, thinking the man would have need of its additional warmth. Finally, she curled herself as best she could into the rocking chair that was near the bed. David had made this chair and she had made the cushions—and now she was using it to sleep in because a strange man was in her bed. No, not strange. He was as familiar to her as Michael. Odd, she thought muzzily, as she, too, drifted into a light sleep.

She was not sure what wakened her. There was no sound in the room but the soft hiss of the floor heater. Throwing off the light blanket she looked towards the bed to check on her patient and was off the chair in a flash. He was lying on the bed with the bedcovers thrown to one side, his legs half over the edge as though he had tried to get up and had passed out. He was unconscious and shivering. Taking the blanket, still warm from her body, Carolyn threw it over him. Then putting his feet back on the bed, she added his own covers.

The room was not cold. The floor heater was not large but it warmed the room. For someone the size of the sergeant, the cover he was under should have been more than enough. But he continued to shiver under his layers of blankets so violently that the whole bed seemed to shake with him.

Carolyn had earlier put his thermal shirt in front of the heater, thinking he might need it later. Now she grabbed it up and yanked it over his head, rolling his body this way and that to get it on as quickly as possible. There was no time for gentleness. His shivering worried her as much as his fever had. She covered him again and going to the chest, took out the extra blankets and covered him with those, also. She was really frightened now. 'Come on, Sarge,' she begged, her voice ragged in her anxiety, 'You were so hot earlier. Where is it now?' His skin felt cold and clammy, like death itself. Hastily she pushed that thought aside.

What to do? Quilts and blankets didn't seem to be the answer. The only solution that presented itself seemed to be right out of Hollywood. But what else? The sergeant continued to shiver, his face grey and pinched, his lips bloodless with a faint bluish tinge. Carolyn made up her mind. Maybe it's become a cliché because they know what they're talking about, she thought as she hurried to wake Michael.

'Mike, wake up. I need you.'

'What?' he squeaked sleepily.

'Come *on*!' and she ran back to the bedroom without waiting to see if he was coming.

She pushed at the man until he was on his side and then led Michael, who had been at her heels, to the side of the bed the man was now facing. 'He's too cold,' she explained rapidly, 'and we've got to warm him up quickly. Now get in and put your back next to him. Let him curl around you, like having a hot water bottle.'

Michael climbed into the bed as he was told and Carolyn watched him get into position. 'Golly, he *is* cold!' he exclaimed, for the man exuded no warmth of his own and his chill seemed to pervade even under the blankets.

'I'm going to get in on the other side,' Carolyn told her son, 'and do the same as you. Hopefully, we'll make him so warm he'll think he's a toasted cheese sandwich.' Michael giggled softly. Suiting action to words, Carolyn curled herself around the man's back and buttocks. She threw one arm as far as it would go around his torso and allowed her hand to rest on Michael's shoulder. Please, let this work, she prayed silently. She shivered a little herself as the man's chill seemed to reach right through the fabric of her clothing so that her own body heat became lost in it.

She felt stiff and awkward and slightly silly as the man trembled against her, but apparently they had done the right thing as gradually his shaking lessened and then stopped altogether. Carolyn began feeling a warmth not coming from her own body as the man slowly relaxed, leaning slightly against her. Raising up on one elbow she saw that he seemed to be once more sleeping naturally with one arm holding Michael, also sleeping soundly, in the curve of his body.

We look like pieces of an interlocking puzzle, Carolyn thought wryly, but she kept her position, afraid to move just yet. In a while she began tentatively throwing off blankets, one at a time, to make sure the sergeant could maintain his body temperature. Her fear disappeared as she continued to feel his warmth and she knew that now she could safely leave his side. She would get back into the rocking chair in just a minute but would leave Michael in the bed. The thought of the rocker was not appealing. She was very comfortable.

She lay reviewing the events of the past several hours, wondering what the morning would bring, but worry and exertion caught up with her and she, too, slept. She did not know when the man shifted position in his sleep but she shifted hers to match it as naturally as if she had been sleeping with him for years. The wind howled and snow drifted against the cabin but the three of them lay in a deep cocoon of sleep, each giving warmth and comfort to the other.

When a large hand cupped her cheek Carolyn awoke abruptly. Her eyes flew open and she found herself looking into a pair of heavily lashed, drowsy brown eyes only inches from her own. 'Hello, sweet Carolyn.' The words might have been the sighing of the wind so softly spoken were they, before the thick lashes again slowly descended and the man's breathing was more more deep and rhythmic. But Carolyn had watched, mesmerised as his fascinating mouth had formed the words and she couldn't have moved or spoken if she had tried, so startled was she. How did he know her name? Who *was* he?

She took his unresisting hand from her face and placed it gently on the pillow between them, then eased herself from the bed. She was still fully dressed and felt grubby and dishevelled but over all she was frantic to know who was sleeping in her bed—this stranger who didn't *feel* like a stranger, who knew her name when she didn't know his, and who made her constantly want to touch him, giving her feelings she had not had for another man since David. She couldn't understand herself and she resented this man for making her feel this way.

Cold grey light was coming through the windows and the room was icy, for the floor heater had consumed its fuel and had automatically shut itself off. Carolyn slipped her feet, still in her warm woollen socks, into a pair of moccasins and put a floor length bathrobe on over her clothing. She would have to get the fire going in the sitting room. The fireplace was fitted with a device that spread its heat throughout the cabin.

Her hair was styled for the minimum of care and all it took was a quick brush to get it in order. She was tall but slightly built, with small breasts that gave her a boyish look in the jeans that she favoured. She was quite unaware that her rounded, feminine buttocks that swayed with unconscious grace as she walked belied this image she had of herself. A pair of slightly tilted blue eyes dominated a small heart-shaped face, but when she saw herself in a mirror she first saw her nose, too long she thought, and her mouth too wide. She wasn't really pretty, but neither was she unattractive. Throwing another puzzled glance at the sleeping man, she gathered up a change of clothing and left the room.

Carolyn's thoughts seemed to run in circles as she went about her early morning routine, building up the fire, heating water for what this morning would be a quick sponge bath, putting the coffee on. It wasn't until she sat at the table, nursing a steaming cup of coffee and gazing out the window at the still blowing snow that she thought of his wallet. Of course! His driver's licence would tell her who he was!

She hurried into the bedroom, gave a quick look to

make sure the man was still sleeping and quietly took
the wallet from his hip pocket of his jeans. Her hands
shook and her knees were like jelly. She felt like a thief.
It was, of course a silly feeling. What she was doing was
perfectly logical under the circumstances, but there was
something rather horrible about going through another
person's things without their knowledge. She sat down
shakily in the rocking chair before opening the wallet.

It was curiously flat, as though empty, but when
Carolyn opened it with trembling fingers, several
hundred dollar bills dropped into her lap. She scarcely
paid attention to them, looking for something that
would identify the man in her bed. There was nothing—
no driver's licence, no credit cards, no papers of any
kind. There was nothing but the money and a picture of
herself as she had been ten years ago.

The snapshot was from her waist up and she was
standing on the front porch of her parent's house in
Texas. She wore a joyful, triumphant smile and was
holding high for the camera to capture, a brand new
baby Michael. She remembered this photo well for she
had had several copies made for family and friends. Her
father was an amateur photographer and she had
thought he had caught on film exactly her thoughts and
feeling on her first day home from the hospital with her
new baby.

Turning the picture over she read the words she had
written so long ago: 'Our love is with you always,
wherever you are.' Carolyn's eyes filled with the tears
she hadn't shed in a long, long time. This was the
picture she had sent to David. How had this man come
to have it? The picture's creases now exactly fit those of
the wallet that had carried it and its worn and frayed
edges testified that it had been carried for several years.

Seeking an answer, she looked towards the man on

the bed and was startled to see the stranger raised on one elbow, looking back at her. And he *was* a stranger, for the eyes that she thought she knew so well had gone flat and hard so that his face was now changed completely. She was too agitated to wonder at the change now and she whispered without preamble, the photo clutched to her breast, 'Who are you?'

'It's a long story,' he answered coldly. 'Do you make a habit of going through your men's pockets?' He made it sound as if having strange men in her bed was a common occurrence.

'I was looking for identification,' she found herself answering defensively in spite of knowing she had nothing for which to apologise. She was too surprised by the intended insult to even respond to it.

He quirked a derisive eyebrow and Carolyn's patience snapped. 'Look,' she said, 'believe what you want,' and her tone made his insult seem petty so that he flushed slightly. She put the money back in the wallet and laid it on the bedside table. 'I want to know who you are and I want to know where you obtained this picture!' Her voice was forceful and not a little angry.

For a fraction of a second his lashes came down to hide his eyes but when he looked back at her they were as hard and opaque as before. He lay back against the pillows. 'As I said, it's a long story. Let it wait awhile.' On the other side of him, Michael was lifting a tousled sleepy head.

' 'Morning, Mom,' he greeted her, yawning hugely. 'How's the sergeant?'

'He seems to be recovering,' his mother answered drily. 'Why don't you ask him?'

Michael, sitting up completely now, looked fully into the man's face. 'Hey, are you okay?' he asked seriously.

'Yes, Mikie, I'm fine,' he was answered just as seriously, and the man reached out to ruffle Michael's hair with a look of supreme satisfaction on his face. Carolyn noted that he also apparently knew Michael's name at the same time another part of her was aware that his eyes were now as warm and deep as she remembered. She was surprised at the small pang of regret that they hadn't looked at her like that.

'Sorry about taking your bed,' he was telling Michael. 'I hope I left you enough room.'

'Oh, it's not my bed. It's Mom's. I was just your hot water bottle,' the boy grinned. The man lying beside him looked to Carolyn for enlightenment.

'You took a chill,' she told him stiffly, 'and we couldn't get you warm enough. Michael went into the bed with you to give you some body heat.'

The man gave her a long look as if suspecting that she was withholding something before turning to Michael. 'Well, you were a good hot water bottle, Mikie. I'm as warm as toast.'

'As a toasted cheese sandwich?' There was a wicked grin on Michael's face as he winked at his mother.

'As a toasted cheese sandwich,' the man confirmed, but his look was puzzled.

Carolyn stood abruptly before Michael could explain the joke. 'You need to be up and dressed, young man, and the sergeant needs to rest.'

'That's the second time you've called me sergeant. Why?' Again, the opaque brown eyes reached out to touch her, but their touch was not gentle.

'Because you ordered us to,' Michael giggled before Carolyn could answer. 'You were so funny! You thought we were in the army and you were ordering us around.' He giggled again, but sobered on instant of remembering. 'You grabbed my mother and shook her,' he added as he once more searched the man's face seriously.

A spasm of pain contorted the man's face for a moment as he turned to look more closely at Carolyn. 'I'm sorry, Mikie. Please believe that. I wouldn't hurt your mother for the world.' Though he spoke to Michael, his eyes never left Carolyn's face and she felt sure that every inch of her had been examined. She felt herself colouring under his scrutiny. 'Did I hurt you?' he asked quietly.

'Of course not,' she lied and flushed even more as a mocking eyebrow went up. 'Time to get dressed,' she ordered Michael, as much to get the man's attention off herself as anything, but her son was obliging and after favouring the sergeant with a forgiving grin, bounced off the bed. Carolyn ushered him out the door and then turned to the figure in the bed. 'Could you eat some scrambled eggs?' she asked in a stilted voice, not like her usual vibrant one at all.

'Sounds good. I'll be there.'

'Oh, but you shouldn't . . .' she started to protest, startled that he would even think of getting up after the horror of the night before.

'I said I'd be there. I feel fine!' His voice had a definite edge to it and giving a slight shrug Carolyn left the room, closing the door quietly behind her.

Her mind was in a turmoil. Instead of answering her questions, he had added more. How and why did he have their picture? He knew both their names and yet she had not signed the photograph, merely dated it. His attitude towards her this morning was one of anger, bordering on the downright insulting. Why? And now he was in the bathroom—had gone right to it without asking directions—another mystery. Her mind kept coming back to a possible answer, but such an outrageous, unpalatable answer that she dismissed it almost as it took form.

He was coming into the kitchen area now, wearing his jeans and socks but still in the thermal shirt she had so roughly put on him in the night. Now that he was on his feet she noticed again how big he was. There was not a spare ounce of flesh on him and yet his build was massive.

'Do I smell coffee?' he asked now, putting a hand out to grasp the back of one of the kitchen chairs with seeming nonchalance.

'Yes,' she said, 'but I fixed tea for you.'

He frowned. 'I'd rather have coffee,' he told her shortly and a lesser person than Carolyn might have wilted.

'I'm sure you would,' he was answered sweetly, but Carolyn wasn't giving an inch. 'Perhaps later,' she modified with a glance at the mutinous set of his jaw. 'And you had better sit down,' noticing that he had a death grip on the back of the chair and was as white as his shirt. He gave her a long look that she returned until the humour of the situation could no longer be totally suppressed. 'Please.' Sweetly spoken, but her dancing eyes that had the look of her son's, made a lie of the polite smile that accompanied the request. He dropped rather hard into the chair.

Carolyn wondered at the stamina that even now allowed him to sit without falling over. She didn't know what his ride up the mountain had been like but just since she had seen him, his body had taken a beating. He was still running a fever. His eyes were overbright and he was much too pale under his tan, though his cheeks had an unhealthy flush. She noticed as she sat a plate of scrambled eggs and bacon before him that his hands were trembling slightly as he drank his tea.

'Where's Mikie?' he asked.

'Bringing in some more firewood.'

'You let him go out in *that*?' He was incredulous, looking out the window at the thickly blowing snow. It was the first time anyone had questioned her decisions concerning Michael and Carolyn wasn't sure she liked it.

'The wood is right beside the door,' she explained reluctantly. 'We dropped it there last evening when you appeared,' and as if on cue, Michael came through the door in a swirl of snow, his arms laden with kindling.

'Hi, Sarge,' he greeted and to his mother, 'Breakfast ready?'

'Ready when you are,' she answered, hurrying to close the door behind him.

Michael dumped the wood in the woodbin, quickly shed his outdoor wear and hung it on the peg before washing his hands at the kichen sink and taking his place at the table. 'Boy! Am I starving!'

'I know,' his mother answered straight-faced, but with a twinkle, and set a plate of bacon and eggs in front of him, then fixed a plate for herself. Michael ate with his usual good appetite and she, too, was hungry, but she noticed that the sergeant was eating very little. Finally he gave up the effort and put down his fork.

'Guess I'm not as hungry as I thought I was,' he said. 'Sorry.'

Carolyn, too, put down her fork. What a stubborn, exasperating man! Couldn't he see that he had done this to himself? 'Of course you're not hungry. You *are* still running a fever and you've worn yourself out just coming to the table,' she said bluntly. 'Why don't you get back to bed and I'll bring you some aspirin before that fever goes any higher?' She rose from the table.

The man stayed where he was. 'I told you I feel fine,' he said evenly, looking up at her.

'What you tell me and what you are, are two very different things,' Carolyn said, letting her exasperation show. 'I'm not blind and if you're honest, you know you feel like hell and are as weak as a kitten.' Then, feeling a blow below the belt was necessary, she added, 'You gave us a terrible time last night. There is little reason to put us through it again. That fever of yours is frightening,' she glanced significantly at Michael, 'and I have very few medical supplies.'

He started to say something, his eyes unreadable, but Carolyn was already feeling slightly ashamed of herself and made a small concession. 'If you don't want to be in the bed, you can rest for a while on the couch in front of the fire.' She didn't realise that there was a hint of pleading in her own eyes.

Michael, who had been taking in this exchange, grinned at the sergeant. 'No one wins an argument with Mom,' he said somewhat proudly.

Carolyn flushed, but the man smiled slightly. 'So I see,' and then grudgingly, 'All right, I'll rest on the sofa, but I feel *fine*!'

He stood, but shakily, and Carolyn feared for the chair he was hanging on to so tightly. Noticing her look, he let go of it and turned towards the couch wearing a look of grim determination. Carolyn knew that she dared not help him, but she signalled slightly to Michael, who was anything but slow witted. Leaving the table quickly, he said with his usual good humour, 'Let me help you, Sarge,' and the big man smiled down at him and placed a hand on his shoulder.

Carolyn gave a mental shrug. He would respond to Michael but he wouldn't respond to her. Why should she care, she thought, as she poured water that had been heating on the stove into the dishpan. She didn't know anything about him and he knew a darn sight too much about her. He could be a crook out to make mischief, but even as she thought it she knew it wasn't so. He was stubborn, short-tempered, and suspicious but he wasn't out to hurt her or Michael in any way. It was strange that she knew this with certainty when she didn't even know his name.

She finished washing the dishes and went into the bedroom to change the sheets and remake the bed. Michael usually helped with all the household chores, but Carolyn thought it was better that he keep the sergeant company this morning.

With the bedroom tidy once more, she knew that she could not put off another confrontation with the sergeant any longer. He was still a very sick man and she doubted that she could pull him through another attack if his fever raged as it had the night before. She didn't like playing the role of clucking mother hen to this man but he left her with no choice. Aspirin was the only weapon she had in her tiny arsenal and, for it to effective at all, he would have to take it soon, before the fever once more escalated beyond control.

As she approached the pair with thermometer and aspirin in hand, she relished the sound of their voices forming a soft chorus with the crackling of the fire and the moan of the wind in the quiet cabin. Michael was sitting on the floor beside the couch, telling the man resting upon it about their struggle to get him through the snow and into the cabin. 'Then,' he laughed, 'you stood up and walked in, all by yourself, saying, "Let's get inside," ' his voice dropped to a deep, false baritone, 'just as if you had walked the whole way!'

The sergeant laughed with him softly, if ruefully. He seemed embarrassed by the incident.

'I hate to break this up, sergeant, but I'd like to take

your temperature before giving you this aspirin,'
Carolyn said matter-of-factly, bracing herself for battle.

The man looked at her for a long moment and then,
as if conceding the fight, said quietly, 'I don't need your
aspirin.' Before Carolyn could protest, he continued,
'I'm aware that my temperature is too high, but I have
medication for it in my saddle bags.' He stopped talking
abruptly and closed his eyes, looking exhausted.
Carolyn and Michael stared at each other dumbfoun-
ded. Why hadn't he said something before?

'Are the saddle bags in the stable, Michael?' Carolyn
asked.

'No, I brought them in last night,' he answered. 'I
hung them on the pegs with the jackets.'

'That's all right. I'll get them,' she said, as Michael
was about to get them for her. Taking them from the
pegs near the door where hung the jackets, hats, and
their own saddle bags, she put them on the table. They
were surprisingly light, considering how heavy hers
usually were when she travelled up the mountain. The
reason was evident when she opened them. There was
only a change of clothing, a shaving kit, a couple of
books, a leather case of some kind—and under the
clothing a plastic container of pills. Taking it up, she
read the directions, staring at them a long moment
before shaking out the prescribed dosage and taking it,
with a glass of water, to the man lying on the couch.

As she once again approached the pair in front of the
fire, Michael was saying as if the omission had just
occurred to him, 'You know, Sarge, your never told us
your name.'

'This is Mike Flemming, Michael, the man for whom
you were named,' Carolyn answered him, looking the
man straight in the eye as she handed him the tablets
and water.

Mike Flemming's gaze never wavered as it held her own, his eyes telling her nothing. Neither did he speak as Michael spluttered, 'Big Mike Flemming! Wow! But I thought he was . . .' He trailed to a stop, suddenly embarrassed.

'Not now, Michael,' Carolyn said emotionlessly, considering the man's waxen face with a cool deliberation. 'He'll tell us all about it when the medication has had a chance to take effect and he is rested.' Not giving her son a chance for further questions, she changed the subject. 'Will you bring me the piece of needlepoint I finished last time we were here and help me stretch it? It is in the bedroom in the top of my closet. My board is also in the closet, if you will bring it, too.'

Carolyn's eyes had never left the big man's face. Long forgotten hurt and anger were pushing at her, leaving her face a mask of her usual self. When Michael had left the room she said coldly, 'Your name was on the prescription label.' Even to her own ears it sounded like an accusation, but of what, she had no idea.

'It wasn't a secret,' he said evenly. 'I just had no opportunity to explain.' Levering himself up on his elbow, he was obviously expecting a bitter confrontation, an attitude that for some reason defused Carolyn completely.

'I guess not,' she conceded, her anger disappearing as rapidly as it had come. She was even able to give him a small smile. 'Nor is now the time. You need to rest, not talk. We'll leave you alone a while and you can tell us what needs to be told later when you are feeling better.'

In truth, she needed some time to herself. When she had read his name on the prescription container she had not been at all surprised. It was as if she had known it all the time. Still, she needed time to come to terms with the fact.

He sagged against the cushions, as if coming to the end of his strength, and closed his eyes, covering the top of his face with his forearm. The gesture focused her attention on his mouth and she found it looking curiously vulnerable. She fought back a desire to touch it with her own.

She turned and was walking away from him when she heard the merest thread of sound.

'Thanks.'

Never had gratitude been expressed in tones of such infinite sadness.

CHAPTER THREE

SHE went to the kitchen table where Michael was laying out her needlepoint and stretching board and they began working, making as little noise as possible. They talked quietly of this and that, but Carolyn firmly kept the conversation off speculation about Big Mike Flemming. They didn't need to guess now, she said, when they would know it all later.

After awhile she checked on Mike—how easily his name came to her—and found him in a deep, revitalising sleep. Normal colour was already returning to his face but she put a hand to his forehead and then to his cheek to check for fever. As he had last night, he made that small nestling movement at her touch and her heart turned over. He was warm, but not enough to cause her concern. Unconsciously, she closed her fist for a moment as if to keep the feel of his now bristly cheek against her palm.

Covering him with a light blanket, she went to find herself something to read. She knew better than to attempt the Eastern Philosophy with all that was on her mind, and took an Ian Fleming from the shelf. Maybe a little murder and mayhem with Agent 007 would soothe her mind. Michael, too was curled up with a Hardy Boys mystery that had belonged to his father when he was a boy. Like herself, he glanced frequently at the sleeping man. Carolyn knew that, also like herself, he was consumed with curiosity.

Despite her best efforts at concentration and the heroics of James Bond, an old puzzle asserted itself between her mind and the printed page. David, her David who had loved this place as much or more than she, had willed his half of 'their' mountain to the man who now lay sleeping on the couch. Carolyn, even after ten years, still felt shocked and hurt at the very thought of his betrayal and, try as she might, she could not understand it.

In the last six months before he was killed, David had often mentioned 'Big Mike' Flemming. Carolyn could tell from his letters that a strong friendship had grown between the two men, an unusual occurrence, for David, with the exception of herself, was essentially a loner, though he liked people. Because of this, she had been happy to agree when her husband had asked her to name the baby Michael if it was a boy. A month after his request little Michael David Watson had been born.

David had called her as soon as he received the news but the connection had been bad so that she could barely understand him and she had been unable to talk with the Mike for whom her baby had been named. However, she did receive a brief note in an almost indecipherable handwriting that contained a cheque for a hefty amount to start baby Michael a savings account. The note had been signed with a surprisingly legible 'Big Mike'. She had kept the note and put it into Michael's baby book.

Nothing had prepared her, however, when in David's next to last letter before he was captured, he told her that if anything should happen to him he wanted 'Big Mike' to have his part of the cabin and land. His company was on the move and his letter had been brief to the extreme. He had not had time to explain and Carolyn had been horrified.

His last letter, received on the following day, was

again an upsetting one, including a puzzling statement. He had ended his brief letter as usual with a declaration of love for her, but had added after his signature the hastily scrawled postscript, 'Take good care of Mike for me.' Carolyn had never been sure to whom he was referring. His friend had always been 'Big Mike' and the baby 'Michael', though *she* had often called the baby 'Mike'. Surely David had meant the baby. Hadn't he?

She had written back immediately, voicing her questions and hurt but her letter had been returned unopened. She had learned that David was considered 'missing in action' and was thought to have been captured. Anxiety and prayers for his release had overshadowed all else and questions were forgotten as she waited for news.

She waited three months, until one bright summer afternoon an officer from the military had called on her and she had been informed that David's death was now official. He had died in an enemy prison of wounds received when captured. Carolyn had been devastated and even now, felt as if half her soul had died with her husband. In some obscure way, sometimes she felt as if she almost hated him for dying and leaving her behind.

The demands of an eight months old baby eventually pulled her from a self-destroying apathy and she was able to see her lawyer to straighten out David's affairs. It was then that she had learned that David had indeed done as he had said and had left his share of the cabin in the Rocky Mountains to his best friend, Big Mike Flemming. Again, Carolyn had felt betrayal, that her husband would give away a place that had been, to both of them, a part of the heart of their marriage. Carolyn developed a strong dislike for Mike Flemming and it was over a year before she could bring herself to come back to the cabin. However, she hadn't had to share it after all.

Much to her secret relief, that left her feeling more than a little guilty, her lawyer learned that Big Mike could not be accounted for by the military and had been officially listed as MIA—Missing In Action. Two years later, Michael's savings account had again been given a sizeable boost when Big Mike had been declared legally dead and it was learned that Michael David Watson, David Watson's son, was his sole heir. Presumably, Big Mike had no family.

Carolyn had eventually come back to the cabin, had found peace with David's memory here, and had brought Michael with her to share this peace as often as possible. It was accessible only by horseback so that at first she had brought Michael sitting in the saddle in front of her. But he was riding almost as soon as he was walking and was now as adept in the ways of the mountain as she, having learned everything she and the Cub Scouts could teach him.

Carolyn's eyes lifted of their own volition from the book she wasn't reading to the still figure on the couch. Now Mike Flemming was here; he was not dead after all. And she was glad; so very glad! Somehow, after the first initial shock, she didn't mind sharing the cabin with this man. It seemed so . . . *right*. Though she barely knew him, some instinct made her refuse to believe that he would interfere with the serenity of the mountain. Maybe it was because he was sort of like a mountain himself, she smiled to herself, big and silent and, well, reliable.

In the quiet of the cabin, with its silence enhanced by the crackling of the fire, she was conscious of a subtle change that had taken place in the atmosphere between yesterday and today. She couldn't put her finger on just what the change was, but it was giving her goose bumps. Anticipation? Surely not. Yet she felt like tomorrow was Christmas Day and she was ten years old . . .

Unable to sit still any longer she went to the window and stood gazing out at the stark whiteness of the scene. The worst of the storm seemed to be over. The wind had lessened in intensity and it was no longer snowing, at least for now. The surrealistic beauty of the scene fascinated her, as every facet of the nature of the mountain fascinated her. At the cabin she was never lonely, never frightened, never bored.

Feeling a light brush against her arm, she turned her head to find that Michael had joined her and was also gazing at the wonderland before them. 'It's hard to believe that Easter is this Sunday,' he said quietly, not breaking the mood. He stared out the window a moment longer and then said surprisingly, 'Mom, don't things just feel *good*?'

Carolyn looked into her son's young, earnest face before lightly touching his cheek with her finger, 'Yes, they do, Michael,' she said simply. 'I was thinking that myself.'

They continued to stand at the window, her arm about his shoulders, but Michael's stomach apparently couldn't stand the inactivity. Suddenly he announced, 'I'm starving!'

'I'm hungry, too,' Carolyn laughed. 'Come set the table for me and I'll reheat the stew we had last night.'

She retrieved the stew from the cold storage that enabled them to refrigerate many of their supplies. This was another of David's ingenious devices. Earth packed around this end of the cabin almost to the roof provided added insulation to keep out the cold in winter and the heat in summer. David had dug a small hole into this earth, accessible only from the cabin through a shoulder high trapdoor in the wall. He had packed the edges of the small cave with ice that at this altitude seldom melted. As a result, Carolyn had a *cache* for keeping perishables that was accessible to the people in the cabin but not to the 'critters' of the mountain.

'Should I set two places or three, Mom?' Michael asked.

'Three,' came a rumbling voice from behind him. 'I'm so hungry I could eat a horse. I hope you didn't lock the stable door.'

Mike Flemming indeed looked fit, his face now back to its normal healthy tan, his very being seeming to exude animal vitality. He stood massive in his stocking feet, his fingers in his hip pockets, his unfathomable brown eyes warm as he grinned down at Michael.

'I didn't,' Michael grinned back, 'but you'd better hold off on the horse. Mom fixes a mean venison stew!'

'And it's ready. You two wash before you come to the table.' Carolyn found herself smiling happily for no apparent reason.

They meekly headed toward the bathroom to appear a few minutes later fresh faced and damp haired, Mike now wearing the red woollen shirt he had worn the night before.

This time there was no picking at his food as he ate with gusto and obvious enjoyment, polishing off three big bowls of the meat and vegetables and at least half a loaf of homemade bread, all washed down with the milk Carolyn had made up from powder. Michael, no slouch himself when it came to eating, was impressed. 'I don't think I've eaten for a couple of days,' Mike apologised ruefully, catching Carolyn's eye, 'and that was certainly good stew. Venison? Do you hunt?'

'No, this part of the mountain has never been hunted as long as we've owned it. The Richardsons, the couple who stable our horses in the lower valley, gave it to us. There's coffee,' and she kept her face perfectly straight, though her eyes were dancing, 'Would you care for some?'

Mike's lips twitched, but he didn't quite smile. 'Black,' he said succinctly.

As Carolyn poured the steaming, fragrant coffee into thick earthenware mugs, she grinned at her son. 'Your turn, Michael.'

'Yes, ma'am,' he said resignedly. 'Cinderella again.'

'Yep,' she agreed without a shade of remorse, and he began clearing the dishes from the table. 'We can take our coffee to a more comfortable spot, Mike, while this slave cleans up.'

Mike gave the boy a mock-pitying look as he left the table, mug in hand.

They took their coffee to the easy chairs by the fireplace and talked indolently of the weather as Michael washed the dishes. Carolyn knew that Mike was ready to answer their questions but was waiting for Michael to join them. This he did in record time, seating himself Indian style on the floor at his mother's feet, his back against her chair.

'All right,' said Big Mike Flemming, 'what is it you want to know?'

Carolyn didn't hesitate. 'I want to know,' she said steadily, 'how you have in your possession a picture that I sent to my husband.'

'David gave it to me,' Mike answered simply, 'or I think he did.'

He seemed to wince as Carolyn drew her breath in sharply, then began to explain in calm rumbling tones. 'We weren't captured together. David was taken first and a couple of months later they got me. I was moved several times and one of those times I found myself in the same camp David was in. I managed to get myself put into the same cell.'

At this point Mike's story became slow and halting. The detachment with which he had begun disappeared as he brought forth memories that he wished were not a part of his life.

'He was sick, dangerously so. He had been beaten badly several times and some of those wounds didn't heal properly and some remained badly infected. With the conditions there . . .' He left the sentence unfinished. 'I tried to nurse him as best I could but there was little I could do. They wouldn't give me any medicine for him—not even clean bandages.' His voice held a wealth of bitterness and Carolyn knew that there was much he wasn't telling them. He didn't look at her as he talked but gazed into the fire, reliving the horrors of an enemy prison camp in its dancing flames. 'He grew steadily worse. I bribed the guards with whatever I could find or steal that was of value to them to try to get medicines, but I couldn't get enough and the little I could get came too late.' His voice shook with remembered frustration.

'Even before we were captured, David had talked of you constantly, and of Mikie—Michael,' he corrected himself, smiling slightly at the boy. His gaze switched once more to the fire as he continued. 'I heard so much about you that I came to feel as if I knew you as well as I knew David. He told me of your building this cabin together, of your hopes and dreams and plans that went into its construction. Every log of this cabin became familiar to me,' and his eyes flicked briefly—and lovingly—around the room before going back to the flames.

'In the prison camp, David's home and family

became the most real thing to me in that nightmare.' He stopped speaking for a moment and neither Carolyn nor Michael spoke. Tears streamed unheeded down Carolyn's face as this man gave some of her husband back to her.

'David was an excellent storyteller, as you know, and talking of you seemed the only thing keeping him alive. But he kept getting weaker and weaker. One day the guards came with a stretcher and said they were going to put him in a hospital. Before they carried him out, he told me to tell you that it was all right.'

Mike looked at Carolyn as he spoke, his voice flat and emotionless, but a muscle in his jaw pulsed erratically. 'Those were his exact words. "Tell Carolyn that it is all right."'

'What did he mean?' Carolyn managed.

'I don't know. I thought you would. When I went back to my bunk after they took him out, your picture was lying on it. How it got there, I don't know for sure. I always felt that David had somehow left it for me, although in the end he couldn't leave his bunk. I've carried it with me since, as a reminder of him. He was the best friend a man could have. He was the best of men . . . and I loved him.' Again there was a long uninterrupted pause. 'After they carried him out on that stretcher I never saw him again,' he added, almost as an afterthought.

No one spoke for a while, each busy with his own thoughts. Carolyn broke the silence by asking, 'Do you want it back?'

'What?' Mike's eyes swung to her blankly.

'The picture,' Carolyn explained. 'Do you want it back?'

Brown eyes carefully empty of emotion, he gazed at her a moment before answering simply, 'Yes.'

Carolyn rose to go to the bedroom. 'I'll get it.' As she came even with Mike's chair, she touched his shoulder. 'Thank-you,' she said quietly. For answer, he reached up and clasped her hand tightly. She stood there a moment, her hand under the warmth of his soft grip, each of them feeling keenly their mutual loss. Then Carolyn gently withdrew her hand and continued into her bedroom.

Once there she slowly closed the door and leaned against it as tears washed over her face. It was like having to face David's death all over again, only now she knew what it was to live without him, something she hadn't believed could be borne ten years ago. Loneliness that she had thought long conquered welled up in her as pictures of her laughing, visionary husband rose from their resting place to gently touch her closed eyes.

David, who had loved philosophy and puns and babies and fast cars; who had faced life with a mixture of earthiness and sensitivity and always led with his chin. He had been a laughing man, but with a deep streak of practicality that had protected them both from the many curves that life can throw. Though a confirmed dreamer, he had always planned ahead. How she missed him! Yet Mike somehow made his loss so much easier to bear, possibly because he missed David as much as she.

Carolyn's mind refused to imagine David dying in the steaming filth of a jungle prison, his laughter and vitality diminishing steadily day by day. Long ago she had set her mind to remembering him as she had known him, not with the horror that newspaper accounts had presented of Asian prison camps that now were more than confirmed by the scars on Mike's body. She wanted to remember David as joyous and free on this mountain, for she knew with certainty that if David's spirit was still on this earth it was here, not in the jungles of Southeast Asia.

Behind her eyes, David, his wheat blonde hair ruffled and shining in the thin mountain sunlight, threw her his lopsided grin and winked. Carolyn smiled back. I love you, David, she told his memory silently. Thank-you for being the peaceful, giving person that you were. As his vision faded, the tears dried on Carolyn's face and her shuddering ceased as she once more found peace within herself.

Now she was able to think objectively of the sad but beautiful gift David's stories of his family had been to the man who had been incarcerated with him. Though he had not written his novel, still he had woven stories that Mike had not forgotten. It was difficult for her to imagine David as a storyteller. She had never thought of the spoken word as his forté and he had always been extremely reticent about anything personal. Although friendly and outgoing, it seemed out of character for him to have divulged so much of their life in that way. David had always kept special things to himself. She wasn't sure she liked Mike Flemming knowing so much about her life with her husband. Now they were co-owners of the cabin. It would take some getting used to.

Taking the stained and faded snapshot into the living room, she handed it to Mike who slowly put it back into his wallet without a word.

'Where is Michael?' Carolyn asked, noticing the absence of her son.

'He went to shovel a path to the stable. I imagine he needed some time alone, as you probably do. I'll help shovel.' He started to lift his large frame from the chair where he was sitting.

'No, Mike, don't be silly. I'm fine, but thank-you anyway. Will you have another cup of coffee?' He shot her a penetrating look but subsided in the chair before nodding.

She took his cup with her own and went to the kitchen to refill them. We are so disgustingly polite, she thought ruefully, as if we were strangers. Then her mouth quirked briefly in the corners as she caught the absurdity of her thought, but her mind skittered on. Did he honestly believe that she would have him tramping around in the snow and cold after she had battled so hard for his life only last night? Why, she would have to be comatose to do such a thing! He didn't seem to have much faith in his fellow man—or woman. Mike Flemming had to be the strangest thinking man she had ever met.

As she returned with the filled cups she asked a question that had been niggling at her for some time, 'Mike, why did you take so long to deliver David's message and to let us know that you were still alive?'

'I didn't get back to the States until about three years after David's death,' he answered. 'I had picked up this fever while I was in Asia and it took me some time to recover . . . if you can call it that.' Again, his voice held bitterness. 'I was in and out of hospitals for about a year. When I was well enough, I located you in Boulder and flew in. I called your apartment but a babysitter answered and said you were out with your fiancé. Obviously, you had recovered from David's death and there didn't seem much point in raking up old memories, so I left.'

To Carolyn's ears he sounded faintly accusing but, surprising herself, she heard her voice answering the accusation. 'David had been dead four years,' she said stiffly. She didn't like the faint defensive note in her tone. 'We had been happy together. I wanted that happiness again.'

'*Are* you happy again?'

'I didn't remarry, if that's what you mean. But yes, right now I'm very happy.' Hadn't she and Michael just been discussing that very thing?

Something flickered across his face as Mike stood abruptly. Walking to the mantle, he leaned his arms against it, his back to her as he examined the flames. 'Do you have everything you need?'

Carolyn looked at the wide back and brawny shoulders of the man leaning against her mantle. Such bigness and overt virility in a man had never appealed to her, but now she wondered what Mike would say if she answered his question with what she was thinking. What if she said, For some reason, because *you* are here, Mike Flemming, my life is complete for the first time since I lost David. When you walk out that door, you will take a part of me with you. I have no idea why this should be so. I barely know you; I don't understand you; I'm not sure I even like you, though I trust you with myself and my son.

She said nothing, however, and at her continued silence, Mike turned to look at her questioningly. 'Yes,' she answered at last, quietly and certainly, 'I have everything I need.' Neither her voice nor her eyes betrayed the slightest hint of her thoughts.

'Why didn't you marry the guy?'

The question was unexpected and Carolyn gave it some thought before answering, her eyes now on the writhing flames. She sat curled in the easy chair, clad in jeans and a blue pullover sweater that reflected the colour of her eyes, her hair a silken fall to her shoulders. She was the most serene woman the man looking at her had ever encountered, reminding him of a cool, clear mountain lake; yet she was also bossy and exasperating, with the uncanny knack to touching just those areas that stripped him of the peace he had worked so hard to find.

At last, when he was beginning to think she wouldn't answer, she said, 'That's something I've often wondered myself. Steven and I have much in common. We both like the outdoors, books, and so on. He and Michael get along well, and Michael likes and respects him. But something wasn't quite right. I couldn't explain it to Steven at the time and I can't explain it to you now. I broke off the engagement but we still see each other and he is a good friend.'

'This Steven is a fool if he's willing to put up with such a washed-out arrangement. I certainly wouldn't in his place.' Carolyn didn't like the edge of contempt in his tone. What right had he to comment on her friends or her life? No one had asked for his opinion.

She flicked him a glance from the corner of her eye, but her voice was quiet and even as she said composedly, 'You aren't in his place.'

'Nor likely to be, you mean,' Mike growled.

'Nor likely to be,' she agreed. No, this man would be her lover *and* her friend but he would never be her lover *or* her friend. Unbidden, she had a sudden longing to feel that kissable mouth on her own. What would it be like to have Mike for a lover? Carolyn pulled herself up sharply, faintly shocked at the direction of her thoughts.

He stood glaring down at her and she looked calmly back at him, a smile deep in her eyes but not reaching her slightly parted lips. She looks like she's promising everything, he thought angrily. How could this woman be David's wife? 'I'll see if Mikie needs some help.' The anger showed clearly in the set of his shoulders as he went to take his jacket from the peg.

When his hand was on the handle of the door, she called after him, 'Mike, your gloves are on the chest in the bedroom.' He threw her a look that would have nailed her to the wall had she appeared to be paying attention, before striding into the bedroom and coming out a moment later ostentatiously pulling on the gloves. Then he yanked open the door and went out with a bang.

'Whew!' Carolyn said aloud, 'I'm lucky he didn't throw something at me!' and she grinned openly, unsure of the source of his anger, but enjoying it anyway. She hadn't realised she was such a bully, but he was so *easy* to push into anger that some perverse imp kept her doing it.

Her mind clear and relaxed for the first time since the storm, she retrieved her Eastern Philosophy and began to study. She was deep into it when Mike and Michael came laughing through the door. Rather uncomprehendingly, she looked up at their boisterous entrance.

'Oh, oh. Mom's studying again. You can always tell. She gets fog in her eyes. Sorry about the noise, Mom,' Michael apologised.

'Not to worry. Make yourselves a snack, if you want. Not too much, though. Dinner in a little while.' She waved a vague hand towards the kitchen area as her mind returned to her studying.

Their subdued chatter formed a peaceful background as she compared the various paths to Enlightenment taken by those of the Eastern world. Her mind seemed to stretch and expand in a way that it never had before. Her perceptions seemed sharper, her insight more keen. Goodness, she thought, I feel like I'm high on some drug and all because I'm so ... so ... *happy*. There it was again, that elusive feeling that seemed to make her spirit dance.

Glancing at the clock she saw that it was much later than she expected and knew that Michael would be 'starving' if she didn't begin dinner soon. She had taken steaks out to thaw earlier and with them she would fix fried potatoes and open a can of vegetables. It was a heavier meal than she would ordinarily have fixed after having the stew for lunch, but she was afraid anything less would leave Mike still hungry.

As she passed them on her way to the stove she saw that they were deeply engrossed in a chess game. Michael seemed to be playing with more serious concentration than he showed when playing with her. Good. He needed a more formidable opponent than herself to keep him on his toes.

By the time dinner was prepared, the game was over and Michael came to the table very much surprised. 'I lost, Mom,' he said as if he couldn't believe it. 'He beat me without half trying.'

'I was more than half trying, Mikie. You play an excellent game; but you made the fatal mistake of underestimating your opponent. That is something you should never do—not in chess, nor in anything else.' He ruffled Michael's hair to take a little of the sting from the criticism.

'I guess you're right,' Michael conceded, and then grinned. 'But look out next time!'

Dinner was eaten with amicable small talk and Carolyn was glad she had fixed the steaks. Mike finished his off with evident enjoyment and when he complimented her cooking, she told him mischievously, 'I hope you had enough. I'm not used to cooking for a crowd.'

Michael gurgled into his milk and Mike, too, smiled, not seeming to mind that the joke was on himself. 'Well, that steak was a crowd pleaser,' he said, 'and to show my appreciation I'll clean up the dishes.'

'That isn't necessary,' Carolyn said quickly but when he insisted, she compromised. 'Why don't we all do them? It will go faster that way. I'll wash, you dry, and Michael can put away.'

'This is just like an assembly line,' Michael commented as the dishes were passed from hand to hand. He was stretching as far as he could reach to place a serving bowl on a high shelf when Mike took it from him and put it where it belonged with ease.

'That reminds me,' said Carolyn thoughtfully. 'How is it that you are so familiar with where things are in the cabin, Mike?'

'As I said, David told me a great deal, but actually . . .'

'He's the Spirit of the Mountain, Mom!' Michael interrupted excitedly.

Carolyn was so amazed she forgot to correct Michael's manners. '*You* are?' She turned incredulous eyes on Mike.

'I'm not much of a spirit,' he answered with a small, tight smile, 'but I have been coming here for about the last five years. I assumed you knew that David had left me his share of the cabin.'

'Yes, I knew. He wrote and told me he was going to do that, but I never connected our visitor with you. We thought . . . We had been told that . . . Oh, you know,' she ended lamely.

It was incredible! Off and on for the past few years they had noticed signs of someone else having been in the cabin. True to the tradition set by the old mountain men, the cabin was never locked. A fire was always laid, and basic supplies were on hand when they left for the lower valleys. The altitude of the high valley, for they were near the timberline, as well as the inaccessibility of the cabin meant that few people would come this way, but the cabin was always left in readiness for anyone in need. Several times Carolyn and Michael had returned to find their supplies replaced by others, the fire laid in a different manner, or the towels and blankets folded in a different way.

At first, this had made Carolyn nervous, but she hadn't wanted to report it since nothing was ever missing or disturbed, the place was always as clean and meticulously neat as she had left it—and she *had* left the door unlocked. After a while she grew used to the phenomena and had dubbed their mysterious visitor the 'Spirit of the Mountain'. To think that the 'Spirit' had been Mike Flemming!

'But why did you never come when we were here?' she questioned. 'Why did you wait until now?'

'Would you believe that is just the way things worked out? I never planned my visits. I came when I had the chance. You just never happened to be here when I came. As for waiting until now, to be honest, I didn't plan on you being here. I thought I would have the place to myself.'

His eyes were on the plate he was carefully drying and Carolyn thought there was an odd note in his voice. She was at a loss for words, shock warring with a ridiculous feeling of guilt.

Michael had no such problem. 'Lucky for you we *were* here, Sarge, or you might still be lying in the snow,' he said bluntly.

Mike gave the boy a small smile but said nothing, his very silence echoing sickeningly between them. Michael, sensing something wrong, looked up to search the big man's face intently. 'Didn't you ever want to meet us, Sarge?' His voice held a bewildered sadness.

A look of intense pain passed over Mike's face and he turned to wrap the boy in a fierce bear hug. 'Oh,

Mikie,' he growled, 'you will never know how much I've wanted to see you. Since that first picture of you as a baby, I've wanted to know you.'

If possible, he held the boy tighter. Over Michael's head he looked straight into Carolyn's eyes, his own deep and warm and dark. Carolyn, just as she had feared when she had first looked into their endless depths outside in the blowing snow, fell into them now without so much as a token struggle and knew that she was lost.

They stood for a moment in tableau, the boy locked in the man's arms, the woman locked in his eyes.

CHAPTER FOUR

It was Michael who brought them back to earth. 'When we're finished with the dishes, Sarge, do you want to check out my pocket video game? It's great!' and he and Mike began a discussion of the various video games on the market to which Carolyn listened with only half an ear.

She had too much to think about, not the least of which was her foolishness in losing her heart to Big Mike Flemming who, despite his affection for Michael, very obviously did not want them taking up any of his life. She had a feeling that what he had said just now had been said very much against his will, possibly to satisfy a small boy's feeling of rejection. He was holding them at arm's length, answering fully all of their questions but giving very little of himself away. All she really knew about him was that he had been David's closest friend and that the affection between the two men had been mutual. She didn't know where he was from or what he did for a living. Why, he might even be married! That brought her thoughts to a halt.

So flustered was she that without thinking, she broke rudely into the merits of PacMan to ask, 'Are you married, Mike?'

If he was surprised at the question he didn't show it, yet he hesitated before asking, 'No, I've never married.'

Wondering at his moment of hesitation, she pursued incautiously, 'Have you never wanted a wife?'

His eyes turned flat and cold. 'Oh, I've wanted a wife, but she belonged to someone else,' and he turned back

63

to his conversation with Michael, effectively cutting her off.

A flush stained her cheeks but she couldn't really blame him when she had been so rude herself, she thought wryly, staring at his slightly turned and coldly dismissing shoulder a moment. The thought of him loving someone else twisted inside her, bringing unbelievable pain. Yet what pain she must have given him with her thoughtless question.

Finishing the dishes seemed to herald the approach of evening as the last of the light faded. When the lamps were lighted, the cabin took on a warm, comfortable glow but the computer sounds of the video game added a touch of the twentieth century to its old-fashioned atmosphere. Carolyn held a book in her hand, pretending to read but watching and occasionally smiling at the friendly joke-filled rivalry between Mike and her son.

They were all tired, however. It had been a long night and an emotional day. When Carolyn suggested bed, no one demurred.

Mike, when faced with the choice of the couch or a sleeping bag on the floor with Michael, opted for the sleeping bag. 'But,' he warned, 'if Mikie snores, I'm coming in there with you,' and his eyes gleamed wickedly at Carolyn as his mouth turned up into a crooked grin, completely taking her by surprise. Why, he was flirting with her!

'He doesn't snore,' she said hastily, a faint pink in her cheeks. 'At least not very loud,' she amended when she saw the grin on her son's face.

'Ah, Mom! My snoring is not as bad as your grunting in your sleep,' he shot back.

'*Touché*,' she smiled, letting him have the last word. 'Looks like you're better off where you are, Mike. Well, good night you two,' and she bent to give Michael's upturned face a kiss before turning towards the bedroom.

'What about Sarge? Doesn't he get a kiss, too?' Michael asked innocently, but the devil danced in his eyes.

'Yes, what about me?' Mike asked, his voice bland but his eyes throwing a faint challenge.

Knowing there was no graceful way out of it, Carolyn gave in. 'You will have to bend over a bit,' she ordered.

Mike bent his face to hers and as she placed a chaste kiss on his cheek she could feel his rigidity. He hates this, she thought fleetingly, as a muscle leaped in his jaw where her lips touched. No parts of their bodies were in contact, except her lips to his cheek, and yet the atmosphere was charged beyond endurance. It was all Carolyn could do to keep from turning his mouth to hers, but she, too, held her arms rigidly to her sides. They pulled apart slowly, as if pulling against a great force. Carolyn couldn't look at him, sure of the derision that must be in his face. Her emotions clambered so turbulently within her that he must know of the effect he had on her.

'Good night,' she whispered huskily and she fled to the bedroom. Out of the corner of her eye she was in time to see Michael with a satisfied look on his face. Oh, Michael, she thought, you've never played Cupid before. Don't do this to me now.

In the safety of her bedroom she sat down on the side of the bed, her legs like jelly. She was trembling. Hugging her arms around herself, she rocked slightly, appalled. How could she have done this to herself? She, who prided herself on her good, common sense? She had recovered from David's death and it had not been easy. And now she found herself loving Mike Flemming with the same loving intensity that she had had for David, but what a heartbreaking difference! David had returned her love, measure for measure. But Mike . . .

What about Mike? She didn't understand him at all. He seemed to be constantly reaching out to her and then pushing her away. Like that kiss. He had placed her in the position of having to kiss him and then he had acted as if she repulsed him. For a simple little kiss it had had a devastating effect on her. It had been all she could do to keep her hands off him, to keep from kissing him as her heart had suddenly demanded.

When he had looked at her in the kitchen, his arms wrapped around Michael, she had known that she loved him; but it had taken an innocent kiss, no different from the one she had given her son, to make her realise that it was a woman's love she felt and there was nothing innocent about it! For the first time since she had lain in her husband's arms, her body was on fire with love for a man. She wanted to feel Mike's warm body wrapped around her own in this big, empty brass bed. With her head pillowed on Mike's broad shoulder, she wanted to whisper of the weather and school and horses into the comfortable darkness of this room after they had made love. She wanted to feel Mike's breath in her hair as he slept at her side.

Maybe that was why it had never been right with Steven, because she could not even imagine Steven in her bed; but she could imagine Mike and the pictures her mind conjured made her body ache for fulfillment.

Carolyn shook her head at this self she hadn't seen for ten years. Trying to dispel her imaginings, with still trembling fingers she began to remove her shirt and jeans and get ready for bed. She had been so flustered after the exchange in the living room that she had neglected to stop by the bathroom and she wanted to wash and clean her teeth. Not liking the idea of running into Mike Flemming again, she decided to wait until everyone was asleep before making her way to the bathroom for her washing up.

She fiddled around, finding herself little things to do—and keeping her mind firmly fixed on these little nothings—until she judged enough time had passed for Mike to be asleep. Then she hurried through the living room, lit only by the glow of the banked fire, to the bathroom. She didn't see the eyes that followed her progress, eyes that were now neither cold nor hard, but had a smile deep within their depths. Making it to the bathroom and back without incident, she crawled wearily into her bed—that she had shared the night before, she thought with faint yearning—and was instantly asleep.

She seemed to have just closed her eyes when someone was shaking her shoulder. It can't be morning already, she thought as she pulled herself from deep layers of sleep. It wasn't. It was close on to three o'clock and she realised an anxious Michael was standing by her bed. 'What is it, honey?' she asked softly.

'It's the sarge, Mom. I think he's sick again.'

Carolyn was up immediately, pulling on her bathrobe as she hurried into the next room. She found Mike in his sleeping bag near Michael's, tossing and turning, moaning softly in his sleep. Bending down she placed a hand to his forehead but his temperature was as it should be.

She turned to Michael, hovering anxiously at her shoulder. 'It's all right,' she whispered. 'Only a bad dream, I think. Go back to bed. I'll stay here a few minutes.' She watched in the darkness as he crawled back into his sleeping bag to lay on his side anxiously watching her.

Mike suddenly flailed an arm out, muttering and tossing his head from side to side. Carolyn would have been knocked flying if she had not quickly ducked. She caught his big hand in her own small capable one and held it fast. 'Hush now, Mike,' she said softly, as if to a child. 'It's all right. Hush now.'

She had read somewhere, and found it to be true with Michael, that the dreamer would usually 'dream the terror away' if not awakened during a nightmare. Mike now seemed to cling to her hand as she talked to him softly and soon the dream apparently played itself out. Michael, too, was asleep once more. With her free hand she pulled the edges of the sleeping bag up over Mike's shoulders where it had slipped down and then, obeying impulse, kissed him softly once more on the cheek, but this time the touch of his rough face against her lips lit no fires, leaving her merely at peace. He didn't stir, but as she went to pull her hand from his, he gripped it convulsively. Again she tried to pull it free and this time he let it go.

In her own room again, Carolyn lay a long time gazing into the darkness before she, too, slipped back into sleep. When she awoke later it was to the smell of coffee in her nostrils and with the invigorating feeling of being rested.

Carolyn sat up and gave a luxurious stretch. The room was still in darkness and her bedside clock said almost six. She bounded out of bed, slipped on a clean pair of jeans, a shirt, and a bright red cable-knit pullover. She felt terrific today! The sun was going to shine and she wanted to see it. Humming to herself she quickly pulled on thick socks and her western boots then ran a quick brush through her hair before grabbing up her knitted cap and gloves and leaving the room.

The living room was still in darkness except for the one lantern turned low in the kitchen area. She could see Mike in silhouette standing at the stove. She didn't speak but hurried to the bathroom to splash her face with icy water.

Reappearing, her cheeks glowing, she made her way to the kitchen area. 'Good morning,' she whispered softly so as not to awaken Michael who still slept wrapped in the cocoon of his sleeping bag.

'Good morning.' Mike, too, rumbled softly. 'Do you always get up this early?'

'Nearly always. I'm a day person and I especially love mornings. The sun is going to shine today. Would you care to join me in taking in the sunrise?'

'You sound positive.'

'I am. I'm never wrong about sunshine. Want to bet?' and she gave him a mischievous grin.

He raised one arm as if to back off. 'Oh no. Forewarned is forearmed,' he quoted. 'I never bet against a sure thing.'

At her questioning look, he said succinctly, 'David.'

Carolyn could find nothing to say so she gave a resigned shake of her head. David seemed to have left out very little.

She shrugged into her jacket, as did Mike, pushed her hair up under her cap, and poured herself and him a cup of coffee before pulling on her gloves.

Together they went out into the cold, crisp darkness, the stars still twinkling icily overhead, but the first red and yellow streaks of the dawn beginning to appear over the far mountains. While Carolyn held his coffee, Mike brushed the snow off the bench that was next to the cabin wall, built so long ago by David for this very purpose. He had never shared her sunrises, however, preferring the warmth of his blankets as long as possible. She and Mike now sat without speaking, each wrapped in the beauty of a Rocky Mountain sunrise. The dawn soon drove the stars away and when the fiery glove of the sun had cleared the mountains, Carolyn let out an unconscious sigh.

She took a sip of her forgotten coffee, found it cold, and poured it into the snow. 'Always happens,' she said ruefully. 'I should know better by now.' Mike laughed softly and poured his own cold coffee into the snow.

They continued to sit quietly as the sun strengthened. Carolyn broke the silence. 'Mike,' she began tentatively and then hesitated unsure of how to go on.

'What do you want to say, Carolyn?' he asked. It was the first time he had consciously called her by name and she felt a little thrill of pleasure at the sound of it on his lips.

The thrill was submerged, however, in what she felt compelled to say. 'Last night you said that you had not planned on us being here. Does it bother you not having the cabin to yourself? Because, if it does,' she said in a little rush before he could answer, 'maybe we could draw straws or something to see who goes. I'm not unselfish enough to leave without a fair draw just because you've come,' she smiled slightly, 'unless, of course, you have a real problem you need to sort out and can't stand company.' What must he think? None of what she had said had been what she had wanted to say at all.

She had been looking at her hands as she talked and now she looked up to find him looking at her strangely, almost she thought, with an expression of pain.

'Did you take your medication this morning?' she asked quickly and he gave a small snort of disgust.

He didn't answer either question but instead asked one of his own, his eyes now on the far mountains. 'When David wrote to you that he was leaving me half the cabin, how did you feel?'

Carolyn didn't answer right away, but when she did it was with honesty. 'Shocked. Hurt. Like he was giving you half of our private lives.'

'And now that you know that I'm alive and you have to share the ownership?' he pursued, turning toward her to look at her intently.

Again she was honest. 'At first, I resented you. I didn't like the idea of sharing—and it really is a strange thing for David to have done. But now ... well, I suppose I've become used to the idea.' What an understatement!

His eyes left her face as if accepting her answer and focused on his hands as they turned his empty coffee mug over and over. 'Do you want me to leave and come back when your stay is over?'

How could she answer that, Carolyn wondered. He had given her no clue about his own wishes. Of course she didn't want him to leave, but she didn't know how to tell him that. Finally, she threw the ball back into his court. 'I asked you first.'

'Hell!' he said in exasperation, getting to his feet abruptly. 'If you can stand me, I can stand you.' He waited until he was at the cabin door before adding, 'Besides, your cooking is just a little better than mine.'

Carolyn sat for awhile thinking over that incredible conversation. She still had no clear idea of whether Mike wanted them here or not. Well, she wasn't going—not without a darn good reason. He hadn't given her one and she had given him every opportunity to do so. He hadn't exactly welcomed their being here, either, however.

As for herself, she was glad he was going to stay. It would give him a chance to get to know them, to get to know *her* and maybe like her. He certainly didn't seem too impressed as yet, certainly. She had a sudden wish to be prettier and able to say all the bright, witty things the books said men liked.

She had never had to worry about how to approach David. From the time they had met there had been immediate rapport. Both of them had known right away that their lives were irrevocably tied. Though she felt this now with Mike, he quite obviously didn't return the feeling.

Carolyn gazed at the tops of the far off trees, not seeing them, trying to orientate herself to what, for her, was a unique situation. She had never in her life wanted to attract and hold a man's attention. Loving and being loved by David had been as natural as breathing. She hadn't thought about it or worked at it. Then there was Steven. He had been attracted by her but she had not put herself out to get his attention. She had never consciously dressed to please him nor sought for conversation to capture his interest. She had merely been herself and he had been interested.

Mike made her feel like a teenager again with her first crush. It was a horrible, insecure feeling: wanting to be noticed yet feeling gawky and awkward when she was; longing for the opportunity to talk and then not knowing what to say; looking for ways to make him admire her and then not finding any. She had never realised that stalking one's quarry could have such pitfalls, and she had never in her life seen herself in the role of huntress. Yet how she longed for Mike to love her.

Didn't he know that was what he was *supposed* to do, she thought with self-directed mockery, then sighed deeply. Mike Flemming treated her like a flea in a blanket. He didn't think about her much and when he did it was with irritation. And her foolish heart had given itself to *him*! She wondered what the woman he had loved—still loved?—was like, and her first encounter with jealousy shook her with its green destroying flame.

Carolyn gave herself a little shake. She couldn't change her basic personality; she just wasn't made of the *femme fatale* stuff. She felt no desire at all to change Mike's. Big, brooding, angry and vulnerable as he was, she loved him. If he never loved her she might as well accept the fact and face her life being forever incomplete. She had paid a terrible price to learn that she was a survivor but she dreaded having to pay that price again. Loneliness was a bitter coin. She couldn't stop the little spurt of satisfaction, however, that he was going to stay with them a while. Though she longed for a more intimate relationship, just knowing that he was close and within her care satisfied a part of her. It wasn't enough, not nearly enough, but it was so much better than nothing. On this thought, she went indoors.

She found Mike in the middle of making pancakes— flapjacks, the early mountain people had called them. These almost covered the plates he was putting them on. Michael had already tucked into a large stack of them but took time from his enthusiastic eating to say, 'Almost as good as yours, Mom!' Pancakes were his favourite breakfast.

Mike, too, smiled at her, though she noticed that the smile didn't reach his eyes. 'Never let it be said that women have a monopoly on good cooking. Sit down and let me show you that the battle of the sexes should never be fought over a stove.' He set a plate down at her place with a flourish. It was stacked almost as high as Michael's.

Carolyn sat down readily as soon as she had removed her outdoor things. 'They look delicious,' she sighed, 'but no matter how good they are, I can't eat this many,' and she eyed the tall stack of pancakes in dismay.

Mike looked from her to the plate in front of her and shook his head. 'No wonder you're so skinny, lady. Okay, I'll take two of them but you eat the rest—all of them!' Carolyn was learning when not to argue.

He forked two of her pancakes on to his own plate and added four more from the griddle before sitting down to add butter and syrup lavishly. With the side of his fork he cut a portion and was about to put it in his mouth, when Carolyn had a sudden thought.

'Did you take your tablets this morning, Mike? You never answered me before.'

Mike put down his fork abruptly, his eyes chips of brown ice as he glared at her. 'That's surely my business.'

Carolyn wouldn't be sidetracked. 'Did you?' she persisted.

The man looked at her for a long considering moment and then turned to Michael. 'Mikie, your mother and I are going to argue. But don't get excited, okay?'

'Okay,' Michael said, grinning broadly, his face full of merriment. Arguments weren't so bad when you were prepared for them. This one looked to be interesting.

'Now,' Mike's voice was grim as he turned to Carolyn, 'I said it was none of your business.'

'I say it is.' Her voice was equally grim as she looked him straight in the eye. 'The directions on your medication said it should be taken once a day, before breakfast. If you haven't taken it you are asking for trouble. When one of us is sick we are all affected.'

A note of appeal entered her voice. 'Don't you understand? The same goes for just about everything: happiness, anger, sadness, anxiety. You aren't alone here. The cabin is small and some things just can't be kept to ourselves or ignored by others in such a small space.' She looked at him anxiously, not liking the idea of offending him or appearing to be pushy, but his bout with such a high fever had frightened her badly.

Mike looked back at her, his eyes still cold and hard yet curiously seeming to devour her face. Her hands were clenched in her lap as she held her breath. 'Very well,' he said at last, 'I can see your point. No, I haven't taken the pills, but I will.' His voice was heavy with resignation. 'Just don't keep on about it,' he added and there was threat underlying his tone. 'I wouldn't want you to put yourself out nursing me back to so-called health.'

At that Carolyn dropped her eyes to her plate, swallowing the lump in her throat. That wasn't what she had meant and he knew it. Or did he? Was he trying to put the worst possible light on what she had said, or did he really feel that his illness had been a resented inconvenience? She was at a loss to understand his apparent low opinion of her.

She spoke very little after that, forcing down as much of her breakfast as she could manage. Her appetite had completely disappeared. Eventually, she left half of it saying only that she wasn't used to such large portions when Mike raised an inquiring eyebrow. Neither he nor Michael seemed to have any trouble with their appetite, however, each of them polishing off another helping with several glasses of milk.

With breakfast over, she left Michael to do the dishes while she made her bed and generally straightened the cabin. Mike said something about the horses and went outdoors.

Carolyn eyed the growing pile of dirty laundry and knew it would have to be washed soon, but she would wait until the weather warmed a little so that she could hang it to dry outdoors. Many times the sitting room had been hung with towels and sheets draped over racks to dry because of bad weather but since the temperature would be above freezing tomorrow and the sun would shine, she could wait. Besides, it was a chore she hated since all the washing had to be done by hand.

There were some parts of primitive living she didn't like at all, she thought with a grimace. A washing machine was awfully nice for large, cumbersome items. However, she could do the smaller items today, things that could be hung to dry in the bathroom.

She gathered her own underwear and shirts as well as Michael's and took them to the kitchen that Michael had just vacated. He was in a rush to join Mike outdoors. Carolyn wondered if Mike needed his things washed out but not for worlds would she ask him. He would probably bite her head off! He had, however, left one of his shirts hanging on a hook in the bathroom. That one she wouldn't have to ask about.

She rinsed out the clothing and hung it to dry on lines strung in the bathroom. Thank goodness for wash and wear. Ironing wasn't much of a problem, though she had an iron that could be heated on the stove for any needed touch ups.

The washing had taken up quite a while and she wondered what Mike and Michael were doing so long outdoors. Looking out the window, she saw them in the clearing rolling an enormous ball of snow. A snowman!

She hadn't made one in years, not since Michael had been much younger and couldn't make his own. Her eyes sparkling, she put on her outdoor things and went to join the fun.

'Come help us, Mom!' Michael shouted when he saw her coming from the cabin. Mike said nothing but Carolyn pretended she didn't notice his lack of invitation.

'We'll have to make a good one,' she laughed. 'I'm afraid today will be his only day and probably he's the last of his family until next year.'

'In that case, this will be a snowman *par excellence*,' Mike said and proceeded to be the guiding force in making the biggest snowman Carolyn and Michael had ever seen. When the body was completed, only Mike was tall enough to make the face. Using weather-darkened twigs broken from nearby branches he created, with deft, sure fingers, a quite life-like face for a snowman. Michael ran back to the cabin to get an old straw stetson left over from the summer.

With the hat in place, they all stepped back a few paces to admire their handiwork. Looking at it, Carolyn suddenly drew her breath in sharply, her eyes widening. But it was Michael who put her thoughts into words. 'It's you, Sarge!' he shouted. 'You've made yourself!' Seen at a distance, the shadows merging with the twigs on the face of the snowman caused the face to take on Mike's features. The mouth was thin and straight, as Carolyn had so often seen it directed at herself; the nose blunted, the eyes haunted. Strange. She hadn't consciously recognised that expression in Mike's eyes and yet on the snowman it was familiar.

Turning, she looked into the face of the living man to see him gazing at his likeness in the man of snow, no expression at all in his own face. 'That's me, Mikie . . . a big, overgrown snowman,' and he laughed. To Carolyn's sensitive ears the words were ambiguous and the laugh hollow. She longed to wrap her arms around him and hold him close and make the pain that she knew instinctively was at the core of him go away.

Instead, she said lightly, 'How about some hot chocolate, you two? Such cold creativity needs some warming up.'

Michael's response was enthusiastic and he raced toward the cabin leaving Mike and Carolyn to follow more slowly. There was a short silence before Carolyn said tentatively, 'You seem to have a talent, Mike.'

'For trouble, you mean?' He cocked an eyebrow at her.

She laughed softly. 'No, I mean for making faces. Do you sculpt?'

'Not in the true sense of the word. I'm a woodcarver—as a hobby, that is. It's not the way I make my living.' That explained the leather case in his saddlebags. It must contain wood carving tools.

'Why, you did the carving on the mantle!' Carolyn exclaimed. On one occasion a couple of years before, she and Michael had returned to the cabin to find a wood carving placed on the mantle. It was of a wood duck just lifting from the water. Its wings were outspread, its neck stretched to seek the sky; but one foot was not quite out of the water of a placid lake. All of its yearning for the sky seemed to be in the upward thrust of its body and yet its love for the earth a part of that one downward foot. The wood duck pulsated with joyous life, each feather so finely etched it seemed to quiver in the air. Carolyn had loved it and had blessed the 'Spirit of the Mountain' for this thing of such exquisite beauty.

'You have a very real talent. That carving is one of

the loveliest of its kind that I've seen. Have you ever considered working professionally?'

Mike seemed to withdraw into himself. 'I've never had the time,' he answered shortly. 'It takes time to get established and money to live on in the meantime.' Invisible shutters were closing his face and Carolyn knew he had said all he was going to on the subject. Silently they crunched through the snow, but for once, it was surprisingly a comfortable silence.

Going into the cabin they found Michael getting down the mugs, having already put a kettle of water on to heat. Some years before, Carolyn had been given a recipe for a hot chocolate mix that could be made in huge batches from cocoa and powdered milk. Mixed with boiling water it made up a thick, creamy hot chocolate that held no trace of 'instant'. In its dry form, it could be stored indefinitely in an air-tight container and was ideal for use at the cabin.

Seeing that it was so close to noon, Carolyn made up some grilled cheese sandwiches to go with the hot chocolate for a quick lunch. After such a vigorous morning they all ate with gusto, Mike and Michael joking back and forth and Carolyn joining in their laughter.

Her laughter was soon turned to dismay. She knew what was coming as soon as she heard Michael ask with a grin, 'Were those sandwiches warm enough for you, Sarge?'

Mike, not seeing the joke but knowing there was one somewhere, answered with a smile, 'Sure were.'

Turning to Carolyn, Michael chortled triumphantly, 'Looks like we did it, Mom!'

'Oh, Michael,' was all she could whisper as, her cheeks a fiery red, she stood and began clearing the table with assumed nonchalance. Her hands busy with plates and cutlery, she said sternly, 'Don't you have something you need to be doing, young man?' There was no trace of a smile in her face or in her voice.

Michael, puzzled over the failure of his joke, looked uneasy. 'No, I don't have anything to do,' he frowned, obviously perplexed.

Mike looked from Carolyn's embarrassed face to Michael's puzzled one and asked quietly, 'What's the joke, Mikie?' giving him an encouraging smile.

Michael looked at his mother but she was looking at the table as she picked up the dishes. He knew she didn't want him to continue with this, but there was no way he could get out of it. He was beginning to feel awful!

'Well,' he said hesitantly, 'On that first night, when you were so cold and Mom couldn't get you warm . . . well . . .' he said again, now looking at the tablecloth and outlining its pattern with a finger, 'I got into the bed on one side of you and Mom got on the other side and she said we would make you as warm as a toasted cheese sandwich. And we did,' he ended a shade defiantly, looking at his mother.

Mike, too, was looking at Carolyn, a strange expression in his eyes, but Carolyn didn't see it. She had turned her back on them to make up the dishwater. She was acutely embarrassed and didn't know what to do or what to say, so she kept herself busy and said nothing.

Michael's fingers still traced the pattern on the tablecloth and he watched them intently as the silence stretched. Mike's big hand reached out and covered those restless small fingers but his eyes were on Carolyn's back when he said with unmistakable sincerity, 'You did warm me, son, when I thought I would never be warm again. I thank you both.'

Carolyn's hands went quite still in the dishwater,

though she kept her back to him. She seemed not to breathe. Michael, however, gave Mike's hand a hard squeeze.

Mike, his head tilted slightly and his eyes still on Carolyn's back, said again quietly, 'Carolyn, I said thank-you.'

She remained still as a statue for a breathless second before turning her head and looking at him over her shoulder, her blue eyes darkened to smoke. 'You're quite welcome,' she managed to get out, then turned back and began washing dishes as if her life depended upon it.

A smile touched Mike's mouth and Carolyn, had she seen it, would have found his mouth once more infinitely kissable. 'C'mon, Mikie. Let's see if I can still beat you at chess,' and they left her to her thoughts and to the dishes.

Michael, before leaving, came up to her as she was standing at the sink and gave her waist a little hug. 'I'm really sorry, Mom. I didn't mean to embarrass you or anything,' he said contritely.

'I know you didn't, honey, and I suppose in all fairness, I shouldn't say things that I don't want repeated. Run along now and don't worry about it.'

CHAPTER FIVE

ALONE, she thought about this latest episode as her hands mechanically continued with their task of washing the dishes, wiping the counter, the table, the stove. She hadn't expected Mike to be so *nice* about this. His knowing that they had shared a bed, for whatever reason, had left her wide open to snide and possibly off-colour remarks, yet he hadn't pressed his advantage. True, Michael had been present, but he was young enough that much innuendo passed right over his head. Michael had started the whole thing as a joke in the first place and Mike could very easily have continued with it at her expense. Instead, he had expressed his gratitude for her care.

That was something he had never done, even though one would have thought it was basic good manners. Mike's manners were excellent in every other respect, yet her part in caring for his illness always seemed to make him angry.

Anger. There was a key word. Carolyn frowned at the thought of it. Mike's illness had made him *angry*. Why? From the label on the pharmacy bottle Carolyn had learned that he was to take one tablet before breakfast every day. The prescription was open-ended so that it could be refilled several times before Mike had to see a doctor again. Apparently, Mike had to continue with this medication for some time. What was wrong with him?

The fever had been virulent, had raged almost beyond control, yet the pills had worked a minor miracle and checked it immediately. She shuddered to think what might have happened had the pills not been effective. Had Mike not been taking them before he came to the mountain? She would probably never know. Mike certainly wasn't going to tell her. He was only taking the medication now because of the moral blackmail she had blatantly used on him.

She drained the dishwater and began drying the dishes and putting them away. That had rankled! Carolyn smiled grimly to herself. He hated taking those pills but he hated even more her seeing him weak with fever and having to care for him. That was probably the only reason he agreed to follow the prescription's orders.

Well, she hated seeing him weak with fever, too ... but not because she was inconvenienced by caring for him as he seemed to think. Because she loved him she couldn't stand for him to be ill, or hurt, or angry; and he seemed to be all those things—except when he was with Michael. Even then, she had the impression that he was only just holding those strong emotions at bay for a while. She would almost give her soul for his face to relax into lines of complete contentment as they had for that fleeting moment when he was lying in the snow.

'If you rub that plate any harder, you'll wear a hole in it,' rumbled a deep voice. Carolyn was so startled she dropped the plate, and it would have shattered on the floor had not Mike deftly caught it and put it away. 'What were you thinking of so hard? Your face was as wistful as a little kid looking in a candy store window. Or maybe you were thinking of David?' His voice held a tinge of something indefinable.

'No,' she said, 'I miss him, of course, but I know I can't have him back again.'

'Oh, yes. I forgot,' and this time there was an open

sneer. 'Good old Steven. Decided he might be good husband material after all, hmm?'

'Actually,' said Carolyn stiffly, her eyes snapping defiance, 'I was thinking how nice it will be to have sunshine and warmer temperatures tomorrow. I have quite a large wash to do and I want to hang it outdoors. Did you want something?'

At her words, Mike's face instantly shuttered but his answer was prosaic enough. 'Just came to see if there was any coffee left from this morning.'

'There isn't,' Carolyn answered, 'but I'm finished here now and will make some.'

'I'll do it myself,' he said curtly, without thanks, and proceeded to fill the coffeepot with water.

'Suit yourself,' she said with the most saccharine smile she could find. 'I would love a cup when it's ready.' She hung her towel on the rack and delighted in the scowl that Mike now wore. She left him to it without another word, thinking what a marvellous weapon turning the other cheek could be.

Later, when she was ensconced in her favourite chair once more studying, he brought her a steaming cup and set it on the table beside her. 'No cream, or sugar?' he asked quietly. She smiled at him vaguely, her mind on Confucius and gave a brief negative shake of her head, before once again going back to her book. She didn't see the knowing smiles exchanged between the man and boy, but she thought she felt the lightest touch on her hair before she was once more engrossed in her subject.

The afternoon passed uneventfully, though there was a small flurry of excitement when Mike and Michael came in from feeding the horses. Carolyn was preparing dinner and they talked of tracks seen in the snow near the stable door.

'It was Old Joe, Mom!' Michael said excitedly. 'He

had to have some some time today because the tracks weren't there this morning.' 'Old Joe' was the name they had christened a brown bear they had been seeing in the outlying area around the cabin on and off for years. His tracks were distinguishable because of a toe missing on the front right foot. He had never bothered them in any way though they had been careful to give him a wide berth even when he was seen in the distance.

'He's never come so close to the cabin before,' Carolyn now said rather anxiously.

'This has been an exceptionally hard winter,' said Mike, 'and food must be pretty scarce. If, as you say, we're going to have a thaw tomorrow and warmer weather will be here to stay, then we probably don't have anything to worry about. Bears don't especially like being around people, either, you know,' and he smiled reassuringly.

To Carolyn, however, that smile was one of male superiority and she said rather shortly, 'Of course I know that, and we have always stayed out of his way. But still, to my knowledge, he had never before come into the cabin yard.'

'Then we'll just have to hope your weather predicting ability is up to standard,' Mike's tone, too, was brusque as he removed his outdoor apparel and stalked off to wash for dinner.

Male chauvinist, Carolyn thought crossly as she set the table. Then she smiled ruefully to herself. She just wasn't used to someone's opinion other than her own where events in her life were concerned. Perhaps she had some listening to do also. It seemed with Mike, her feelings were always on her sleeve. Though she accused him, in her own mind of course, of being super-sensitive, she was not her usual levelheaded self, either.

* * *

Carolyn awoke suddenly, and automatically looked at the glowing face of the clock at her bedside. Two-thirty. She slipped quickly out of bed, shrugging into her robe as she hurried with bare feet into the sitting room.

In the banked glow from the fireplace she could see Michael sleeping peacefully but Mike, in his bedroll beside him, was showing the increasingly restless movements of a bad dream. Carolyn bent down quickly and, as she had the night before, placed her hand in his and began soothing him a low, calm voice. The dream didn't last long, soon smoothing itself out until Mike, too, was sleeping as peacefully as the boy beside him. As she had previously, before leaving him Carolyn placed a feather-light kiss on his cheek, her heart squeezing in a vice of pity—a pity she knew he would never condone nor accept.

Hurrying back to bed, her feet freezing, she snuggled under her warm blankets to lie wide awake and thinking. Two nightmares in two nights. Did he have them every night? She had a good idea now of what was causing them.

The evening before, after the dinner dishes had been washed—by the three of them again—Michael had asked Mike why they had been told he had died overseas. Mike had answered bluntly, 'Because the military thought I was dead.' He went on to tell how he had eventually dragged himself out of the jungle near what had been before his capture, a U.S. outpost. By then, however, most military from the U.S. had gone home, leaving behind only a token force. Fortunately for him a member of that force had been inspecting the area when Mike had stumbled in more dead than alive.

Under Michael's questioning, for Carolyn knew better than to ask anything, Mike expanded on his story. Although he talked directly to Michael his tone of voice did not exclude Carolyn and she made no pretence of not listening. Watching his face as he related events that happened between seven and ten years ago, she could tell that to Mike the memories were as vivid as yesterday.

He spoke of attempting to escape after David's death, of being caught and brought back. He had been transferred several times to different prisons, each time taken further behind enemy lines. At one of these prisons, his official identification had been taken from him and sent back to the United States with the message that he was dead. With the hostilities supposedly over by this time, and with no word leaking out that he was alive, the message had been accepted as valid by the military. There had been several more escape attempts until at last he had been successful. He touched briefly on crawling through bamboo jungles, swimming rivers, hiding sometimes just inches from the enemy soldiers seeking him. He told of the rainy season that had probably saved his life by making it more difficult to find him but at the same time had given him the virulent fever that he carried to this day.

'Malaria?' questioned Michael at this point, for he had been reading of the building of the Panama Canal in school and was familiar with the problems caused by that fever.

No, Mike had answered. He seemed to have picked up something that was so rare it hadn't been named. There was no cure and it was only kept at bay by the pills he had to take once a day. The medication itself had come into being as a result of research during his illness.

Mike had said little more and Carolyn knew there was a world of horror he had left unspoken. It had been in his face—in the grim set of his jaw and bitter twist of his mouth. Most all, it had been in his eyes, haunted with remembrance. Mike had not spoken of reprisals for his unsuccessful escape attempts but Carolyn had seen for herself the scars at his neck and wrists and the smaller ones on his upper torso. They told their own terrible story. The scar that encircled his neck was about gone now and in a few years would disappear completely but the scars he carried on his wrists would be there for the rest of his life.

These were scars of the body but the nightmares showed that the scarring was equally deep on the mind. Would he also carry the nightmares with him for the rest of his life—or would peace eventually come to his sleep as time and events created new layers of healing tissue. With all her heart Carolyn prayed that it would.

The next morning she found that she and Mike had established a ritual that they would follow for the rest of their stay on the mountain. Mike had made coffee and together they took a cup with them outdoors to watch the sun come up. They spoke little at these times, letting the benediction of the sun wash over them, but their silence brought them a closeness seemingly denied them in conversation. Mike always went in first and started breakfast while Carolyn lingered an extra few minutes. Each morning Mike's face seemed to smooth itself out a little more, and though by the evenings it had often regained much of its customary closed hardness, slowly he began to relax as whatever demon holding him in its grip was banished for hours at a time.

This morning, as she had predicted, the air was noticeably warmer and Carolyn knew that today she could do the washing. After breakfast she went to the utility closet where she kept the big double tubs she used for washing clothes. It was an old-fashioned affair with a tub for washing and a tub for rinsing. She even had a scrub-board and a hand cranked wringer.

Washing was a heavy, back-breaking job and as Carolyn gathered up all the dirty items she could find she knew there would be no question of being too modest to ask Mike for his dirty clothes. On wash days she washed everything, no matter how lightly soiled, in an attempt to put the next wash off as long as possible. Therefore, when Mike came in from seeing to the horses she asked him for everything that he had that was dirty.

'I'm washing today,' she explained, 'and I like to get it all at one time.'

'I can wash my own clothes,' she was told tersely. 'I saw that you washed my shirt yesterday and, while I appreciate the thought,' a faint curl to his lips made a lie of the words, 'I'm not the helpless male that needs a little woman to take care of him.'

Carolyn's eyes brightened with temper but she answered with enormous control. 'Helpless you certainly are not; but what about helpful? Washing on this mountain is a big job. Water, lots of it, has to be heated and during the wash the water has to be changed often. There is no other way to change it than to pick these tubs up and empty them and then fill them up again. If you want to do all that just for your own few things then I can't stop you, but quite frankly, Michael and I could use some help.'

This stubborn, selfish man seemed to see things only in terms of himself. He apparently had no conception of the word cooperation. Well, she would see to it that he did before he left this mountain again!

She looked at him steadily, her chin out, ready for battle and as steadily he returned her look, his face blank, his eyes unreadable. Then something seemed to flicker behind those eyes and to Carolyn's fascinated astonishment, his face crumpled in all the right places to leave him wearing a shy, rueful grin. (Carolyn would later swear to herself that the pink in his cheeks was a *blush*!)

'You're right, of course,' he further astounded her, 'I've been on my own so long that I forget that work can be shared. What can I do to help?'

By this time, Carolyn's mouth had dropped open in astonishment as she gazed at him, unable to say a word. Mike reached out a lazy forefinger and gently placed it under her chin, pushing her mouth shut.

Her eyes glowed with happiness and her face held a radiance that took his breath away. Surely help with the washing wasn't reason enough for this look of such happiness. His eyes searched her face seeking the cause. 'Well?' he asked, his tone puzzled.

Carolyn took hold of herself. Mike must think her an idiot, but this was the first time he had shown any sense of commitment to the running of the household for *all* their benefits. This was not just a gesture of politeness as was his making breakfast or helping with the dishes. By joining them in this grubby, dirty job of necessity he was making of them a unit, no longer resident and guest. This from a man who, up until now, had shown no commitment to anyone but himself—and even that self-commitment was more than open to question.

'All right,' she said briskly, 'you can start by giving me a hand in getting these tubs outdoors. It is less messy out there even though we have to carry the hot water back and forth.'

Between them, they manoeuvred the unwieldy tubs out into the sunshine and began the tedious job of washing, rinsing, and wringing out. With the three of them working, however Carolyn had never known the job to go so fast, nor to be such an occasion for laughing and joking.

Their laughter rang across the clearing and seemed to bounce off the surrounding trees before drifting on a softer note up into a cloudless blue sky. Carolyn, bending over the tub, the sunshine warm on her back and shoulders, felt happiness rising up and breaking inside her like bubbles of champagne. Looking at Michael, who was making himself a moustache of soapsuds, she felt that he echoed her happiness. Even Mike was wearing that rare look that she loved, his eyes deep and dark and soft, his face content. She tried to swallow a lump in her throat, her eyes filling with tears as they always did in times of deep happiness

At the moment, Mike looked up at her from where he was wringing out the clothes. His eyes immediately narrowed and the smile slid from his face as if it had never been. Under Carolyn's horrified gaze the mask was once more put in place. He lifted an inquiring eyebrow but his eyes had become wells of sadness. She knew that he thought she was remembering David and shook her head mutely, a futile gesture that Mike did not see, his attention once more on his task.

How could she explain that her tears had been tears of happiness, not tears of sorrow; that David was gone and his memory should not be allowed to cloud the pleasure of the day for either of them? She suddenly wondered if she had not hit upon the reason for Mike's antipathy for her. Perhaps he resented it that she did not still grieve openly for David. He seemed to be looking for a sadness within her that was not there and was angry at not finding it. That Mike still felt David's loss keenly was obvious.

The warmth seemed to go out to the sunshine; the

brightness of the day seemed to pall. They continued to joke and laugh but the jokes were forced and their laughter hollow. Carolyn was glad when they were finished and she was left to hang the clothes while the two cleared away the washing materials.

As she automatically hung the clothes on the line and pegged them she cursed herself for her thoughtlessness. This was the first time Mike had really opened up in their presence and she had ruined it by going all teary and giving him a false impression of sadness that had immediately passed itself on to him.

How could she let him know that while she had loved David, he was gone and she had accepted it, as must he? She knew now, where she had not before, that she could love again wholeheartedly. Mike had shown her that. But she was caught in the dilemma of letting him know she *could* love without letting him know that she *did* love. She felt that he was as wary of her as a wild animal to a sloppily baited trap.

How it hurt to feel herself so repugnant to him. Was her attraction to him so blatantly apparent? She hadn't thought so, but then she had never played this waiting game before. Was her body sending signals that she was unaware of? She had been told after David's death that having been married, she would continue to have sexual needs, but she had not found it so. She missed having sex with a man, but as a wild fulfilling expression of love. If the man wasn't right, however, sex seemed to have no meaning in her life. Only with Mike had the physical aspect of love once more reasserted itself. Was she somehow communicating this need to him?

The way she felt now made her relationship with Steven seem so innocuous. Poor Steven. Though he had made tentative advances, she had gently rejected them and he had never pursued the matter. She wondered now that he had been so easily put off. On reflection, Steven was an unknown quantity. Either he was rather lukewarm in his affection for her or he was a better friend than she had thought. She was beginning to see that the fault in their relationship lay solely within herself. She had always seen Steven as a friend first. A lover? Well, perhaps someday. And Steven had never pushed a change in her perceptions.

She could not doubt his virility. Only a little above average height, his body was lean and fit from a life spent in the outdoors. His rather ordinary face was deeply tanned and set off by a pair of denim blue eyes that always seemed to be looking into tomorrow. As an ecologist at the same university where she taught, he shared with her a love of the wilderness. He had remained a friend even after she had broken their engagement, though he was now dating other women on occasion. All in all, he had treated her with a rare sensitivity that she was only now appreciating.

The mountain was at work again, teaching her a lesson in friendship, the clear mountain air seeming to sweep out the cobwebs in her mind. As she hung the last sheet, she was once more smiling. She had gone from worry over her relationship with Mike to a new understanding of her friendship with Steven. Give the mountain time and it would clear up all problems. Perhaps it could even heal Mike.

She was once more at peace with herself as she looked around with loving eyes. The sun glittered on the fast melting snow and here and there new grass was pushing through; even one or two wildflowers was shyly pushing forward. Spring was rushing upon them and the mountain seemed ready to burst with the joy of it, for this year spring had been a long time coming. The winter had been unusually long and hard in the mountains and now the lesser vegetation seemed anxious to make up for lost time, the trees that were not evergreen covered with buds.

Carolyn, too, seemed ready to burst in the joy the mountain exuded. She picked up the now empty laundry basket and twirled it and herself around, revelling in the promise of the spring morning.

Suddenly she froze, her eyes riveted to the ground. There, starting to melt around the edges, were the tracks of Old Joe, clearly visible in the snow here at the far end of the cabin near the clothes lines. Her eyes followed the tracks where they continued across the clearing heading towards the forest. Her heart beating erratically, she turned to see where the tracks had come from but in that direction the snow was crossed and recrossed with their own comings and goings.

Could these be the same tracks Michael had told of seeing yesterday? She hurried to the cabin to find out.

Carolyn found Mike and Michael in the middle of a chess game but when she told him of the tracks they went back with her to investigate.

Mike, squatting on his haunches and putting his fingers in one of the tracks, looked up and confirmed her fears. 'Nope, these weren't made yesterday. I'd say Old Joe passed through here sometime after we had our coffee this morning and before we brought the tubs out.'

Feeling her blood run cold, Carolyn gasped, 'Do you mean while we were in the cabin?'

'Probably looking for breakfast,' Mike agreed, watching her carefully, his own face expressionless. 'There is a chance, with warmer weather coming he won't come back.'

'It's difficult to tell what bears will do. They are so

unpredictable. I just hope he doesn't decide to make this a part of his territory,' Carolyn said worriedly.

'Maybe he just wants to sample your cooking, Mom, before he decides,' Michael grinned.

'Michael! This is a serious matter and not to be taken lightly,' Carolyn reproached him.

'There is no point in getting excited before we know anything.' Now Mike was reproving. 'All we have to do is check out the area before leaving the cabin. We have a good field of vision,' and his eyes swept the clearing between the cabin and the forest. 'If we just exercise a little caution there should be no problem. Now,' he suddenly grinned, 'I left soup warming on the stove. Who's hungry?' He gave Michael a playful punch on the arm.

'I'm starved,' answered Michael on cue, as he ran towards the cabin door.

Walking back with Mike, Carolyn turned once more to look over her shoulder at the tracks in the snow. They seemed enormous.

'They look even bigger because they're melting,' Mike answered her unspoken thought.

'I know. I'm being silly. I just don't like to think of a bear being so close to the cabin, especially when we are inside and don't know he is out there,' Carolyn acknowledged with a shiver.

Unexpectedly, Mike wrapped his arms around her and pulled her close to him, giving her a gentle hug. Carolyn was too startled to resist had she wanted to, which she didn't. Her hands were in her jacket pockets, Mike's hug preventing her from taking them out. Just for a moment she allowed herself the luxury of laying her cheek against his broad chest. In the silence of the clearing she could hear Mike's heart beating a tattoo and knew that its rhythm matched that of her own.

She sighed deeply, as if she had come home after a long absence. Feeling Mike's hand gently touch her hair, she raised her head to look at him. What she saw in his face stopped her heart before it began beating again crazily. His mouth seemed drawn to hers like a magnet and she just as naturally raised her own to meet it.

'Come on, you two! I'm starving!' Michael's young voice shattered the moment. Carolyn felt Mike immediately stiffen. His arms dropped slowly to his sides but it was the mental withdrawal that hurt. His expression didn't alter but Carolyn knew that he was as far away from her as ever.

'Shall we go inside?' he asked formally, as if their shared moment was a polite exchange between acquaintances.

Carolyn's head came up and her chin went out at his cold, off-putting attitude. 'By all means,' she answered with equally stiff formality, her eyes shooting sparks. Then, to his utter surprise, she tucked her hand through the crook of his elbow and walked with him through the cabin door like a queen to a state dinner. Let him be Master Prim and Proper. She could jolly well play lady!

She missed completely the wink Mike shot at Michael over her head but she did see Michael's answering grin and then she just couldn't help it—she had to giggle. At that, Michael, used to his mother's not always conventional ways, burst out laughing and, after a second or two, Mike joined him, his laugh a deep muted infectious roar. It was a little rusty perhaps, as if it didn't get used often.

Carolyn's heart warmed at the sound of it. We'll make him into a human being yet, she promised herself and when Michael caught her eye, she felt his thoughts were much the same as her own. Mike didn't seem to know how to have a good time in ordinary, everyday living. Hadn't he laughed much before he came to the mountain?

'Well, milady, will you join us for a light repast?' Mike asked with exaggerated formality, his eyes actually twinkling as he waved her towards the table with a low bow.

'Delighted, I'm sure,' she answered with an equally deep curtsy, her own eyes dancing. 'If you will give me a moment to ... uh ... . freshen up?'

'But of course, madame,' and he once more made a courtly bow, quite gracefully for a man of his size. Carolyn exited with as much pomp and circumstance as jeans and western boots could command.

Catching sight of her reflection in the bathroom mirror brought Carolyn up short. Her cheeks were rosy with laughter, her eyes glowing with happiness and excitement. She knew what caused that excitement; she only hoped Mike did not. 'Oh, Lord,' she moaned softly, 'I look absolutely besotted.' No wonder Mike was stand-offish around her. She looked positively head over heels in love with him. She was, of course, but she didn't want to *look* it. The thought was a sobering one, causing her to lose her sparkle. Mike, by his own admission, was in love with someone else. You had better back off, lady, she chided herself and straightened her shoulders and her demeanour before leaving the bathroom.

To her relief, when she joined the others at the table the game appeared to have died a natural death and her quietness during the meal caused no comment.

She practiced being circumspect all afternoon as Mike and Michael did several odd jobs around the cabin. She deliberately put on her best 'teacher face', as Michael called it, whenever they asked her opinion on this or that. Several times Mike looked at her oddly and she dared not catch Michael's eye for fear of the façade cracking completely.

That evening, as the three of them sat before the fireplace after the dishes were done, conversation flowed easier than ever before. Mike seemed genuinely interested in their lives and under his gentle prodding Carolyn and Michael told him of their life in Boulder. Asked about her teaching, Carolyn told of being offered a teaching fellowship as she completed work towards her doctorate degree in Eastern Philosophy but Mike could tell that her greatest source of pride was Michael's placement in classes for the gifted students. Her fingers drifted to her son's hair, wheat blond like his father's and as unruly. He was once more sitting on the floor leaning against her legs as they talked. His placement had come because of his ability in chess, she explained and added that few adults had been known to best him. 'Of course, he is just a big frog in a small pond, as you have shown him,' she smiled at Mike, pulling a strand of Michael's hair gently.

At her words he looked up and grinned. 'Rrribbit,' he croaked and she laughed.

Mike put a hand to his head and seemed to wipe his brow. 'Whew. For a while there I thought you had forgotten how.'

Carolyn looked at him blankly for a second before a slow blush stained her cheeks. Then she, too, laughed softly at her failure at sobriety and dignity. 'Where did you go to school, Mike?' she asked in a not-so-subtle change of subject.

'If you mean college, I didn't. I grew up in Chicago and sort of went to high school there. I say "sort of" because I was truant more often than present. Finally, I quit altogether and joined the military as soon as I was old enough.'

'Didn't your mother get mad?' Michael asked with awe.

Dark empty eyes focused on Carolyn's fingers still absently caressing her son's hair as expression was once more wiped from his face. His words were slow and introspective. 'You see, son, we didn't have much money and I had two younger half brothers and a half sister for my mother to take care of. My own father died when I was younger than you are now, and after my mother remarried she had so many to care for that she just didn't have time to worry about a big, overgrown boy like me.' Bitterness and love warred in his voice as he spoke of his mother. 'When I went into the service, I imagine she was glad not to have the authorities knocking on the door looking for me anymore. I had been more interested in running the streets than in being a good son.'

And maybe if she had been more interested in her son, you wouldn't have run the streets, Carolyn thought privately. Her heart went out to the adolescent he had been who had lost his father, but worse, had seemingly lost the interest of his mother. Perhaps that was why he saw his illness as an irritating inconvenience to her.

'Is that when you met my dad?' Michael asked eagerly.

'No, I was in the military ten years before I met your father. I wish I had met him earlier. My life might have been very different. He was a fine man and as close as a brother to me,' he said softly, as though to himself. 'He encouraged me to take the high school equivalency test and then to take a couple of correspondence courses for college credit. I suppose it was David who woke me up to what a joy learning can be. He found everything fascinating and always wanted to know more and more.'

'Do you still live in Chicago?' asked Carolyn into the small silence.

'No, there wasn't really any reason to go back after I left the service. I was at loose ends for a while before I wound up on the Louisiana Gulf coast. I roughnecked there for a time and then started my own construction company, building offshore drilling platforms for oil companies.' He sounded suddenly bored.

'Wow!' enthused Michael, much impressed.

Carolyn's eyes, too, opened wide but for a very different reason. Flemming Construction, out of Louisiana, had made front page news just a few weeks before. It was a corporation dealing not only with offshore rigs, but with all sorts of materials associated with the oil business. It had subsidiaries all over the world. Michael J. Flemming, founder and principal stockholder, had made headlines when he had, with no warning, sold his controlling interest at a considerably lower price than what it was worth and dropped completely out of public view.

Even at that he was several times a millionaire. Yet here he was now, taking his ease in front of her fire after being dragged, more dead than alive, out of one of the worst blizzards of the year, into her cabin. His cabin also, Carolyn amended. So what was this extremely wealthy man doing roughing it on a mountain in the Rockies?

CHAPTER SIX

CAROLYN stood at the sink draining the hot water from the eggs she had just boiled. Tomorrow was Easter Sunday and she and Michael would later decorate the eggs. Michael was too old now to hunt for them but he still enjoyed decorating the eggs, even if he only ate them for breakfast.

Ha! Carolyn smiled to herself. Who was she kidding? She still found as much pleasure in the Easter tradition as any child. Tonight she and Michael would hand paint the eggs as they did every year, letting their imagination run riot. Op-art, pop-art, scissors and glue, or traditional—all schools of thought would be tried. The eggs would be pretty or funny or down-right garish, depending on the whim of the artist. When they were finished they would leave them on the table, but in the morning, before Michael was awake, Carolyn would arrange them in his old Easter basket and leave them in the centre of the table for him to find and admire anew when he awakened. It was a ritual that would probably last until Michael was old enough to leave home.

She gave a little sigh thinking of past Easters when the 'Easter Bunny' had hidden the gaily coloured eggs. Michael's triumphant laughter as he had found each one still echoed in her mind. How she wished she could have had other children, if for no other reason than that the traditions could be shared from child to child as well as from adult to child. Sometimes, even now, her arms ached to hold another baby of her own. The tragedy in losing a husband wasn't just in losing the man.

Placing each egg carefully to dry on a folded dish towel, her thoughts far away, she gave a slight start as Michael appeared beside her leaning both elbows on the table where she worked.

'Shouldn't he be back by now, Mom?' he asked plaintively, rocking one boiled egg back and forth with the tip of his finger.

'Surely not for another couple of hours, honey. It is a good six or seven hour trip down the mountain and even longer coming up,' she reminded him gently. 'And there is an hour's drive to and from the village.'

'Yeah, but he said he would hurry. Seems like if he was hurrying he would be back by now.' He went to the window for what seemed the twentieth time and peered anxiously out.

'You're going to wear a hole in the floor, Mikie. Come sit down and have some hot cocoa. I'll let you try out the cake I baked this morning,'

'Now you're doing it too,' he said ruminatively, as he watched her cut a big wedge of his favourite chocolate cake and put it on a plate for him.

Carolyn licked some of the frosting off her finger tips before asking idly, 'Doing what?'

'Calling me Mikie,' came his now muffled reply, his mouth full of cake.

She froze, and then slowly lowered her finger from her mouth as she looked at her son, a stricken expression on her face.

At the moment they both heard the sound of a horse coming across the clearing. Michael dropped his fork with a clatter and ran towards the door. Carolyn, trying for a little more decorum, wasn't far behind.

She stood in the doorway and watched the rider

walking his horse across the open space in front of the cabin. She had time to admire the way he sat his horse, straight and proud, as though he and horse were one, and the earth was his. She smiled to herself at her fancy. The small smile was still on her face and in her eyes when the rider was close enough to see her clearly, but it died instantly when, having tied his horse to the rail, Mike turned flat, cold eyes on her.

Before she could catch her breath, Michael had hurled himself into the man's arms and Mike's eyes became soft and gentle as they turned to the boy and he returned the exuberant embrace.

For a moment jealousy of her own son welled up in Carolyn, and because she hated the feeling, she turned on her heel and went into the cabin. Neither of them seemed to notice.

She walked straight to the kitchen area and began making coffee. So much for the day's beginning, she thought with unusual bitterness, willing the tears in her eyes not to spill. Her traitorous mind, not obeying her silent orders at all, returned to the dawn.

Last night Mike had informed them that he would be going down the mountain and into the village for supplies. His presence had cut into their stores considerably and supplies were needed. Against all reason, Carolyn had been afraid that he wouldn't come back. She didn't voice her fear, of course, but she hadn't slept well last night. She had spent a restless night calling herself all kinds of fool for acting like a love struck teenager.

She had been up early this morning, but even so, Mike was up before her. He poured her a cup of coffee as she appeared in the sitting room. It was still in darkness except for the lamp in the kitchen area. Dawn was at least an hour away. They did not exchange greetings but sat together at the table drinking their coffee in silence, each lost in his own thought. Mike went out to the stable to make ready his horse and Carolyn began frying bacon that would go on thick slices of bread for Mike to eat on the trail. She wrapped the sandwiches in aluminium foil, her hands busy, her mind a careful blank.

Mike came back into the cabin quietly so as not to awaken Michael, rubbing his hands together. The morning was clear and frosty. As he took down his saddle bags Carolyn thrust the sandwiches into his hands. He looked slightly surprised and Carolyn quickly put her hands behind her in case he meant to give them back to her. 'For your breakfast,' she whispered hurriedly, feeling silly and gauche.

In the dim light and under his hat Carolyn could not see his eyes and an embarrassed flush was pulsing through her face before he replied as quietly as she, 'Thanks. It will taste good later.'

He turned then to go out and she trailed after him to the door, feeling utterly forlorn. With his hand on the latch, he stopped for a heartbeat, his back to her, before turning slowly to face her. As though pulled by invisible wires, his large hand came up to gently cup her cheek. 'I won't be gone long,' he said as if she had asked. Then his mouth brushed hers for a fleeting instant, his eyes never leaving her face. She gazed back at him, knowing her heart must be in her eyes, but totally unable to look away, and felt herself falling into his eyes again and this time perhaps she touched his soul.

Of its own volition, Carolyn's hand had reached up to cradle his face as he still did hers, her thumb making a caressing brush over his cheek bone. She turned her own cheek into his palm for an instant before they both took a small step backwards, partners in a dance in which only they could hear the music.

Without another word Mike had turned and opened the door, closing it quietly but decisively behind him. She had watched through the window as he had mounted his horse and ridden into the semi-darkness, not looking back. She had carried the feel of his hand on her cheek and the brush of his lips on her own with her all day.

Then, just moments ago, Michael had unwittingly shown her how dangerous her feelings were. She had made Mike a part of their lives in so short a time. She was using his terms of expression, thinking him into her tomorrows, worrying about him. She, too, had gone to the windows a dozen times since his departure.

Now this. She couldn't have been told more clearly to keep her distance.

None of her thoughts showed, however, when Mike came in, Michael in tow. She was able to give him a bright empty smile and offer him a piece of cake in a voice that held only the faintest of wobbles. She thought she must be doing well for Mike gave no sign of noticing anything amiss and his eyes touched only briefly on her hands clinching her coffee cup as he told about his trip from the mountains.

The storm of a few days ago had apparently caused havoc in the village, pulling down powerlines and leaving the small community without electricity or telephones for a couple of days. In other areas of the state, motorists had been stranded and one had lost his life when he had left his car in the storm.

Carolyn listened and responded in what she hoped was the right way and at the appropriate intervals in the narrative. But her mind was in a turmoil, running hither and there like a trapped animal. She did feel trapped— trapped by emotions that refused to let her sensible self dictate. Sheer panic rose up in her as she perceived the hopelessness of her situation, causing her to take a deep shuddering breath.

'Carolyn, the storm was over some time ago. No need to panic now.' Mike's voice came to her, a sarcastic edge to it. Some of her thoughts must have shown in her face and she took immediate refuge in anger.

'Don't be silly,' she snapped, glowering at him. 'I was just thinking of that motorist and how horrible it would be to die like that, alone in the snow.' She had said the first thing that came into her head and rose from the table, her head at a proud angle, intending to gather the dirty dishes.

Her face was averted and she didn't see Mike's eyes narrow and turn to brown stones as two bright spots of anger appeared in his cheeks. But she heard the snarl in his voice and her head snapped around. 'If you mean I haven't shown enough gratitude . . .'

Too late Carolyn realised that Mike had taken her words as a reminder to him that she had pulled *him* from the snow. He couldn't seem to forgive her for saving his life. She suddenly realised that this apparent grudge had a great deal to do with his unreasonable anger towards her. She, too, became suddenly and blindingly angry.

'I mean just what I said and no more,' Carolyn cut him off heatedly. Anger became the only way she could release her own uncertainty and feelings of inadequacy that he engendered in her.

'So what if you needed help?' she glared at him. 'What are you feeling so ashamed of? Physical weakness is common to all people at one time or another. It doesn't make you less a man. Nothing can do that to you except yourself. David died sick and weak, but cared for by you, and he was no less a man.'

Mike was on his feet, standing so quickly he knocked the chair over. He had no colour in his face at all now, and Carolyn thought she could see hate written into every line of him. A muscle contracted in his jaw before he rasped in a voice so low and full of menace that Carolyn took a step back. 'Have you *all* the answers, you sanctimonious, opinionated woman?'

Carolyn, now as pale as he, clenched her fists, nails biting into palms. She gave him back look for look, hating him, too, at this moment. 'I wish I did have all the answers,' she ground out. 'You could benefit with a few—as soon as you come down off that elevated plane of yours enough to know the questions.' Tears running down her face from a mixture of anger and deep misery, her back ramrod straight, she walked without haste to her bedroom, and closed the door with extraordinary quietness. There she sat on the edge of her bed and stared at nothing as she allowed the bitter scalding tears to continue with their flood.

Mike stood where she had left him, the muscle in his jaw still working, but the anger in his face erased, replaced by a look of bleak frustration.

'You leave my mother alone!'

Dear God, he had forgotten that the boy was at the table with them. He turned to find Michael glaring up at him, quivering with hostility. Mike put a hand on his shoulder but Michael immediately stepped back causing the hand to fall. 'Mikie . . .'

'Don't call me that! My name is Michael. And you leave my mother alone. You make her cry and she never cries 'cept when she's happy.' He was shouting now, tears streaming unheeded over his face. 'Why don't you go away? We did okay without you. We don't need you!' He began pummelling Mike with his fists, hitting as high as he could reach while Mike stood without moving, his face an ashen mask, doing nothing to stop him.

'Stop it! Stop it, I say!' Carolyn shouted from the doorway. She ran across the room to her son and grabbed each of his flailing arms. Turning him around she hugged him to her where he sobbed convulsively against her, his arms wrapped tightly around her waist.

'Hush, Mikie, hush,' she crooned to him, brushing his hair back from his hot, damp face with a gentle hand. 'It's all right now. Hush.' She did not see the quizzical, puzzled look that Mike shot at her but she did see him as he grabbed his hat and saddle bags and opened the cabin door.

'Oh, no you don't, Mike Flemming!' she flung at him. 'You can't leave him like this. Don't you *dare* walk out that door!'

Mike turned slowly to look at her. She stood clasping the boy to her, glaring at him fiercely. Her face was blotchy from weeping and her eyes red and puffy. Her shining hair was a mess, a tendril clinging to her neck. But her back was straight and proud, her head thrown back ready to do battle. Mike knew when he was beaten.

He turned away from her, giving her his profile as he said in a flat, tired voice to the far wall, 'He doesn't want me here, Carolyn. I've made him hate me.' His face did not change expression with his words but his shoulders seemed to slump with the weight of the saddle bags he still carried.

This was something that Carolyn knew how to deal with and she said gently, her voice full of the loving warmth she could show in Michael's behalf if not her own. 'Mike.' She waited until he turned his head and looked at her before continuing. 'He thinks the world of you. What do you think this is all about? He has never been around two people he loves arguing seriously before, and he doesn't know where to place his loyalty. Wait. Please.'

Mike didn't answer, but he hung his hat and saddle bags back on their pegs and went to the window to stand gazing out. He stood at an angle to her, one shoulder leaning against the wall, his fingers in his back pockets. Carolyn looked at his broad back and gave a little sigh. What a sensitive, complicated man!

As Michael's sobs gradually subsided she held him a little away from her. Taking his chin in her hand she asked, 'Better now?' At his nod, she bent and quickly kissed him on the cheek. 'Go wash your face and then we'll talk.' She gave him a little swat on the behind that brought a shaky smile as he went to do her bidding.

With Michael in the bathroom, she turned to the man still gazing out the window. 'You will have to help me with this, Mike.' He didn't answer or turn around and was still looking out the window when Michael came back into the room.

The boy looked sheepish and slightly embarrassed at his display of tears and Carolyn wondered, not for the first time, why men had to start at such an early age being so ashamed of their more tender feelings. She sat down in her favourite armchair and Michael took a seat close to her at the end of the couch. He kept his eyes fixed determinedly on Carolyn's face, not once looking in Mike's direction. Mike, however, was oblivious for he still had his back to the room.

'First of all,' Carolyn began matter-of-factly, 'I think you owe Mike an apology. Don't you agree?'

Michael was on his feet in an instant, his face incredulous. 'No, Mom. No! He yelled at you. He . . . he made you cry!' Michael looked as if he were going to cry again himself.

Carolyn forced herself not to touch him, not to comfort him. 'Hush, Michael, and sit down. I'm not finished.' His face a study of amazed bewilderment, Michael once more sat down on the couch. His eyes flickered to Mike's broad back and then back to his mother's face.

'What you say is true,' his mother continued, keeping her voice calm and unruffled. 'Mike and I argued. He said some things that made me angry and hurt my feelings and I cried. But you must remember, I said some things that made Mike angry and hurt his feelings, also. The only difference is that he didn't cry.

'But, Michael, the most important thing to remember is this,' and she reached out to lay her hand on his arm, looking into his face earnestly, 'The argument was between Mike and myself. It was really none of your business.' She said the words slowly and distinctly to make her point. 'You had no right to take sides because the argument was not about you. Our argument was no one's business but Mike's and mine.'

Michael still said nothing. He had stiffened at her words but had listened intently. Her voice gentled again after a little pause. 'In this argument, as in most of them,' a slight smile touched her mouth, 'both of us were a little right and a little wrong. Small things were made to seem too important and big things weren't said at all. Then, when you came into it, that made it two against one. That wasn't a bit fair, was it?'

Her son looked at her, his throat working before he managed to swallow his tears. He left the couch and stood before her to say formally, 'I'm sorry, Mom. No, it wasn't fair.' He reached out and hugged her tightly and Carolyn felt her chest tighten with pride.

When he straightened he looked over her shoulder and said in an uneasy voice, 'Sarge, I'm sorry. I had no right to interfere.' As close as he was to Carolyn she could see his hands trembling and held her breath.

'I understand how you feel, Michael.' Carolyn started slightly at the sound of Mike's voice. She hadn't realised that he had moved from his place at the window and was standing just behind and to the side of her chair. 'It is instinct in a màn to protect the ones he loves,' his rumbling voice continued, giving the boy back his damaged pride. He must have made some sign for Michael was immediately around the chair.

Turning sideways, Carolyn could see Big Mike kneeling down, the boy locked in his arms. Mike's eyes closed briefly, and when he opened them again Carolyn thought he had never looked so vulnerable. In his kneeling position their eyes were on a level. He spoke, keeping his arms wrapped tightly around Michael.

'I ask you again, lady. Where do you get your wisdom?' His voice was gentle, completely free of sarcasm, with a curious inflection.

'I love,' she answered quietly and then her mouth turned up in a small smile. 'It is instinct in a woman to protect those she loves.'

Mike reached out his right hand and with no hesitation at all, Carolyn leaned over the arm of the chair and put her own right hand into his big paw. Mike gave a little squeeze and Carolyn knew that never again would Michael be caught between them.

'Now,' she said briskly, though her voice shook slightly, 'I think you have a tired horse outside that needs some attention. Perhaps Michael can help you. I have a meal to begin and need to concentrate.'

'Yes, ma'am,' Mike answered with mock meekness.

'Yes, ma'am,' Michael echoed with the same wicked gleam in his eye.

After dinner that evening, Carolyn put out on the

table the materials they would use to decorate the hard boiled eggs: watercolour markers, glue, glitter, coloured tissue paper.

'What is all this?' Mike asked curiously. 'I thought Easter eggs were dyed.'

'Ah, that's too easy,' Michael answered him. 'We make pictures on ours. C'mon, you can help us.'

'Oh, no. My ears are too short to be an Easter bunny,' Mike teased. 'I'll supervise.'

He stood, leaning with his arms on the back of the chair, as Michael and Carolyn began the yearly and much loved discussion of just how they were going to express themselves in this unique art form. Carolyn at last decided on a garden of purple irises to ring her egg and Michael decided to make his into a bunny face.

Silly talk and gentle laughter and soon Mike was sitting with them at the table. Before long, the pristine white surface of the eggs just couldn't be resisted and Mike was covering one with an army of ladybirds. 'Ladybirds are good for gardens,' he excused himself, glancing at Carolyn's irises.

'Did you have Easter eggs when you were a kid?' Michael asked him.

For a moment Mike's face was shadowed before he grinned and answered, 'Nope. The Easter bunny never could seem to find my part of Chicago.'

Carolyn, afraid that Michael was getting into an area that Mike might not want to talk about, said hurriedly, 'Hand me that yellow marker, Michael. I think my irises need at least one daisy, don't you?' She held her egg up for his inspection.

Michael obligingly gave her egg his full attention and his opinion was that the daisies should have an egg of their own. Mike's wink over the top of Michael's head

made her feel so happy that instead she covered an egg
with happy smiles.

It was three-thirty in the morning and once again
Carolyn's eyes flew open and she was instantly fully
alert. In one fluid motion she had thrown back the
covers and grabbed up her housecoat. She was putting
it on as she hurried barefoot into the sitting room.

Sure enough, the familiar tossing and turning was
coming from Mike's pallet as it had every night since he
had been here. She squatted down and took the hand
that was pulling restlessly at the blankets, beginning to
talk softly and soothingly as she did so. As it had every
night, the hand held hers in strong, firm desperation as
though clinging through a storm-tossed sea. At this
point, Mike would drift into a calmer, more restful
sleep and Carolyn would return to her bed. He never
wakened and in the daylight hours the dreaming was
never mentioned. Carolyn wondered if he remembered
his dreams in the morning or if they only haunted his
nights.

Tonight the dreaming did not ease off. Mike
continued to toss, muttering now about places with
exotic names, his face twisted in anger. Carolyn, afraid
that Michael would wake up, placed the palm of her
free hand on the side of his face, bending low over him,
whispering her message of care, 'Shh, Mike. Hush.
You're home now and safe. It's over. You are free now.
You are home.' At her whispered words he went
absolutely still and Carolyn sat back, her hand still
gripped by his, thinking that now he would drift, as
before, into more peaceful sleep. Instead, she found
herself gazing into wide awake, accusing brown eyes.

'My god, you're not a dream! You're real! What the
hell are you doing here?' His voice was harsh and

dangerous and he looked pointedly where his hand was gripping hers, clutched unconsciously to her breast as she had bent over him.

Her face, still wearing its expression of surprise that he was awake, was now awash with colour. She dropped his hand, her own going to her cheek as she leaned further back, as though his words were physical blows. Her mouth opened but she could think of absolutely nothing to say. She closed it again and, trying to find some dignity somewhere, made to stand up.

Immediately, the hand shot out again and grabbed her wrist. Mike was sitting up now, the blankets falling to his waist, his chest bare and gleaming in the soft glow from the fireplace. He pulled her to him as though unable to help himself, so that from her kneeling position she fell into his embrace, her whole weight landing against him. 'God, I'm sorry, Carolyn. I'm so sorry. I say so many hurting things to you,' he whispered, his face against her hair so that his breath fanned the side of her neck.

Carolyn trembled and without conscious volition her arms came up around his neck to cradle his great head to her. 'It's all right, Mike.' She smiled a little tremulously. 'I mean, it's not all right, but I think I understand a little. I'm a constant reminder of David, aren't I?'

His forehead came down to rest a minute on her shoulder. He said nothing for a space but a shudder ran through his body and Carolyn held him even tighter. When his voice came, as close as she was, Carolyn could barely hear him. He spoke jerkily, with long pauses between each sentence.

'He loved you so. He died having so much to live for. I think the sound of his voice telling me of you and

Mikie and his cabin will be with me forever. It should have been me to die in that hell hole instead of David. He had everything to live for,' he repeated. 'You and Mikie need him.' As softly spoken as the words had been, they contained a wealth of bitterness.

Carolyn laid her cheek against his hair, holding him tighter if that was possible. 'Oh, Mike! No one person is absolutely necessary to another's continued existence. I know now that a person can make it alone if one must, though I would not have said that ten years ago. Don't you see? What "should have" happened, did happen. Believe me, you had things to do with your life, also. I've read of your company's position in the nation's economy, of the endowments you've made, of the children's hospital you've funded. Your own life certainly hasn't been a useless one. Many people owe their lives and welfare to your generosity.'

Mike raised his head to lean his forehead against hers. She couldn't see his face but she could hear the smile in his voice. 'The lady with all the answers—but right now, sweet lady, you don't know what you're talking about.'

She leaned away from him and took his face in her two hands, her face close to his. Without a hint of a smile she said fiercely, 'I know you shouldn't be dead, Mike Flemming,' and she kissed him on his surprised mouth.

'Oh, lady,' he muttered against her lips, wrapping her tightly in his arms almost cutting off her breath, but his mouth was soft and gentle as it met hers, giving her a deep kiss of unutterable sweetness.

Against her will, Carolyn surfaced and drew a little away from him. 'What is it?' he whispered.

A soft chuckle came from deep within her as she whispered in her turn, 'You're breaking my back.'

She clamped a hasty hand over his mouth before he could laugh aloud, though he, too, gave a low chuckle as he shifted her position. She was now sitting on his lap, her back to the fireplace and Michael's sleeping bag, leaning on Mike's shoulder, the top of her head just under his chin.

'Better?' She nodded, not speaking.

They sat quietly for a time, each taking pleasure in the nearness and warmth of the other. Carolyn could hear the steady beat of his heart under her ear. She raised her face to meet his as his mouth once more descended to claim hers. It, too, was a kiss of infinite sweetness—and restraint. Everything within Carolyn wanted more.

Tentatively, her tongue carressed his upper lip, and after the barest pause, it was like touching a match to dynamite. Passion ignited and exploded within them both, whirling them into a vortex that left them oblivious to anything else—except a sleepy voice that came from the adjoining pallet.

'Mom? Sarge' Is it time to get up?'

Mike's hand stilled on her breast, where at some time or another her bathrobe and night gown had been pushed aside to expose its glowing roundness. Carolyn buried her face in Mike's neck. Her back was to her son's pallet and she knew from her position that he could see nothing. His voice, however, had been like a bucket of cold water and with her heart beating like a trip hammer, she couldn't have spoken if she had tried. She left it to Mike, whose heart she could hear beating equally fast. 'It's too early to get up yet, son. I just had a bad dream. Go back to sleep.'

'Okay,' came the sleepy reply and Carolyn could hear him as he turned over and wiggled into a more comfortable position in his bed roll.

Neither she nor Mike moved. Her face remained in his neck, his hand now just under her breast. In the stillness, they heard Michael's breathing deepen into sleep. Mike very carefully began to straighten her nightgown and then her bathrobe. Still Carolyn didn't move. She had the horrible feeling that once they moved apart they might never again be physically close and the overwhelming loneliness of the thought frightened her.

She wanted to suggest they go to the bedroom but she could hear Mike's heart as it once more steadied in its rhythm and she knew the moment was forever lost. Childishly, she continued to sit where she was, hoping that reality would go away. She felt Mike push back her hair and kiss her temple before whispering, 'Hey, lady, are you asleep?'

Carolyn smiled into his neck and kissed it before straightening up. 'Of course I'm awake,' she whispered. 'Look,' she nodded towards the window over his shoulder. 'It's almost dawn. Ready for some coffee?' Her voice was matter-of-fact and she was immensely proud that it did not hint of the bleak hollowness of her feelings.

Mike looked at her for a long moment, his eyes drinking in her face as though he would never see her again. One finger came up to touch her cheek as he said in a voice that in no way matched his eyes, 'Sounds good. You make it this morning,' and he pushed her gently off his lap and on to her feet.

Carolyn went to light the stove feeling as she had when David had been shipped over seas—which was ridiculous when she and Mike were still within the same two-room cabin. The coffee left on the stove to perk, she went into the bedroom to dress, and to use the only method of defence she had where Mike was concerned. She made her mind a blank.

CHAPTER SEVEN

BECAUSE today was Easter Sunday, Carolyn chose to wear a high-necked turn of the century style blouse with leghorn sleeves. There was an edging of lace down the front and she teamed it with a soft denim prairie skirt. She would be mostly in and around the cabin so she pulled on squaw moccasins that came to her knees instead of boots. After using only a minimum of light make-up and brushing her hair until it shone she turned down the wick of the lamp and left the bedroom, carrying Michael's old Easter basket that had been in the top of her closet.

Mike was standing at the table holding a steaming mug of coffee. He lifted one eyebrow, but made no comment on her appearance. Carolyn was not at all surprised when she saw that his eyes were no longer the warm brown wells they had been only a few short moments before. The man in front of her now would not allow himself again to be her lover. Though she doubted they could be friends, she would try.

'It's Easter Sunday,' she said by way of explanation, looking down at herself.

'You look very nice.' He spoke as one trying very hard to meet her halfway and finding the going difficult.

Carolyn pretended not to notice and arranged the artificial grass in the basket before adding the eggs so brightly decorated the night before. Then, taking a big paper maché box shaped like an egg and covered with pictures of Old World fairy tale animals, she opened it and dumped in some jelly beans. She closed it back again and put it beside the basket, stepping back to admire her handiwork.

'Ready?' Mike asked quietly, holding her jacket for her. She shrugged into it, the part of her mind that she allowed to think noticing that his hands never touched her. Picking up the mug of coffee he had poured for her she led the way to the door.

They sat on the bench in silence and sipped their coffee, listening as the birds sang their morning aria to the rising sun. As the sun cleared the tops of the trees Mike spoke quietly, 'Did I wake you?'

Carolyn turned her head to look at him, not understanding.

'Last night . . . this morning . . . when I dreamed. Did I wake you?' He did not look at her but kept his eyes on the distant trees now in silhouette against the morning.

'No, not really,' Carolyn said slowly. 'I'm a light sleeper. You didn't call out or anything. I just knew something was wrong.' She didn't add that most wives and mothers had that 'special ear' for their loved ones.

'You've come every night, haven't you?'

She hesitated before answering, feeling as if in some way she was admitting to a crime. 'Yes.'

'I thought you were a part of my dreams. It's nice to know you were real.' For the life of her, Carolyn didn't know if this was a compliment or a put down.

Not knowing how to respond to this, she made no comment. Instead she asked in her turn, 'Do you dream every night, all the time?'

'Always. Only it is usually much worse.'

They talked no more after that and later, hearing Michael's high, excited voice coming from inside the cabin, they knew the day had begun.

Inside, they found Michael gazing in wonder at the

table for all the world as if he had never seen the eggs before. Carolyn smiled. Easter Sunday was a new beginning for him every year. 'Wow, Mom! We sure did some good decorating! And look at that one. When did you do that one?' and he looked from one to the other of them.

Carolyn looked to see which one he was talking about and caught her breath. In the basket was an egg she had never seen before. She reached out to pick it up and found it as light and fragile as it looked. The raw egg had been blown out of the shell through small pin holes at the top and the bottom, and then the shell had been painted with the water colour markers—but the creator had used such a deft touch that it was hard to believe that the delicacy of the painting could have been achieved using such unwieldy tools. Carolyn held in her hands an exquisite miniature panorama of the cabin washed in the new sunlight of dawn, the trees in dark sillhouette against a pink and yellow sky. A lone mountain stood in splendour behind the cabin and a tiny dot that was somehow a bird flew to meet the new day. Morning freshness radiated from the scene.

Putting the egg back gently with shaking hands she turned to look at its creator, tears streaming down her face.

Mike looked at her with blank dismay and slight anger. Harshly, he spoke, 'I'm sorry, Carolyn. I didn't think.' He lifted one hand to rub the back of his neck in consternation.

'It's all right, Sarge. She just gets weepy when something is beautiful or she's happy.' Leave it to her practical son to explain things.

'Well, which is it?' Mike asked, still with a trace of puzzled anger.

'Both,' she said, laughing through her tears. She

hugged him quickly around his waist, stepping back before he could respond. 'Thank-you so much,' and she hurried to the bathroom to wash her face and pull herself together.

Breakfast was an occasion of laughter, quips, and comments as each chose their favourite egg to eat with bacon and toast. Carolyn chose Michael's bunny face, because she 'always wanted to have rabbit for breakfast'. Michael chose an egg covered with a delicate spiderweb on which sat a dainty and very feminine spider. It secretly gave Carolyn the shudders, though wild horses wouldn't have dragged that admission from her. Michael said he had always heard that spiders were lucky and Mike gravely agreed with him. 'Well, that spider looks positively smug,' Carolyn said.

'So she should be,' answered Mike, contemplating Michael's egg. 'She has a very beautiful web there and should be able to catch any poor fly—especially if it's male.' He didn't seem to see the tongue that Carolyn shot at him. But Michael did and gurgled. 'Do you have a crumb caught in your throat?' Mike asked him solicitously, rising to thump the boy on the back, and even Carolyn could not keep a straight face.

Mike's choice was Carolyn's egg of happy smiles. 'This I know how to deal with,' he said ruefully. Though Michael chortled, Carolyn just smiled and said nothing.

'The other morning . . .' Mike began.

'I was happy and it was a beautiful day,' Carolyn interrupted 'Today is a new day. Let that one go.' She willed him to read a double meaning into her words, her eyes searching his face.

Mike gave her a slow, wicked wink and Carolyn flushed as she smiled a little selfconsciously. She knew that he thought she had all the answers . . . again. She supposed she did sound sanctimonious. It was just possible the world could get along without her advice.

Easter was spent quietly. Because they didn't go to church, Michael read the message of Easter from the Bible. As its reminder of hope was sounded in his young voice, Carolyn, at least, took comfort.

They all helped in the preparations for dinner. Mike had brought the makings for a traditional holiday feast, though they had roasted chicken instead of roasted turkey. The meal was voted a huge success by its participants, each one extolling the virtues of his own particular culinary effort. They were too stuffed for dessert and agreed to postpone the delight of dried apple pie until later in the afternoon.

With the dishes out of the way, they decided on a walk to check on the progress of springtime in their high valley and, incidentally, to work off some of the lingering heaviness of dinner.

The walk was a relatively quiet one as none of them really liked the sound of their voices ringing over the mountain. Carolyn was continually amazed at how in tune with her and Michael, Mike seemed to be. Few of their personal feelings about the mountains had ever been exchanged and yet their approach to nature always seemed to harmonise.

Her thoughts full of wonder at the man that was Big Mike Flemming, she almost walked right into him when he abruptly stopped on the path in front of her. He was looking at slash marks at his eye level on a tree beside the trail. The cabin was easily seen across the clearing from where they were standing.

'He's too damn close,' Mike muttered as though to himself.

Carolyn was competely bewildered. 'Who?'

'Old Joe, that's who,' answered Mike shortly. 'These

are his claw marks and they're fresh. He's marking new territory and he's too damn close to the cabin for comfort. You and Mikie be extra careful from now on anytime you go out the cabin door.'

Carolyn felt her stomach give a little lurch for she knew just how dangerous bears could be.

Michael, true to his boyhood, was more awed than frightened. 'Wow! Look at the height of those claw marks. They're as tall as you, Sarge!'

Mike squatted down in the trail to look Michael full in the face. 'That's how a bear marks territory, son. He's saying this part of the forest is his, and he doesn't want you in it. Furthermore, if he finds you in it he is going to be hopping mad and try to chase you out. It doesn't help that we're right in the middle of what he thinks is his,' and Mike nodded towards the cabin. 'Now anytime you are outside that door I want you to be careful and keep a sharp eye out. Do you understand me?'

The grin was wiped from Michael's young face and he answered as seriously as the man had spoken, 'Yes, sir.' Mike ruffled his hair and stood once more and they continued on to the cabin.

Carolyn could only feel relief as she shut the cabin door, at the same time not liking the idea of not being able to enjoy the outdoors at will.

When she and Mike talked it over later he was of the opinion that, since the bear knew of their residence in the cabin before he had staked his claim, he would not venture too close. 'Now that spring is here, foraging shouldn't be much of a problem. It is very likely that we will never see hide nor hair of Old Joe, but,' he warned again, 'don't forget to look for him!'

That night Carolyn dreamed of David. The dream was

a nebulous one and in the morning she could only remember David's presence, not the dream itself; but she felt as if David was pleased with her and had told her so. She awoke wrapped with his joy, a joy that accepted her growing love for Mike and gave her his blessing. Unconsciously, in the next few days, she spread the loving warmth of her dream over her son and Mike, giving them a time of peaceful harmony.

Following Easter Sunday, the days seemed to pass much too fast for Carolyn and Michael, who would both be going back to school.

Mike and Michael were inseparable and Carolyn delighted in the sight of them together. They constantly had a project going in the cabin and Carolyn had only to mention, to have something put up, torn down, repaired, remodelled or replaced. Mike was teaching the boy to work with his wood carving tools and the clean smell of new wood permeated the cabin. The two often sat in the open doorway, basking in the sunshine, or on the bench outside whittling on some project and talking, the treble of the boy's voice blending with the bass of the man's. Often Carolyn wondered how Michael had managed to keep busy before Mike had come into their lives.

Now, she felt no jealousy of their relationship; on the contrary, it filled her with a deep sense of pleasure. At the same time she worried about Michael's reaction when it came time to leave the mountain—and Mike. They only had a few days left. What the separation would do to her own heart didn't bear thinking about.

Between herself and Mike was a strange friendship, strained to the utmost at times, as close as a heartbeat at others. In the daytime they joked with each other and

teased one another and helped each other. Carolyn lost
the feeling that Mike was keeping her at arm's length as
he began to share with them the give and take of family
living.

Dawn brought them together to pay homage to a
new day and after silently greeting the sun, they
talked—exchanging childhood tales, describing the
events that had caught them up in the last ten years.
They never talked of David and they never talked of
Mike's term of military service.

He did, however tell her of his battles with his fever.
He told of how, following his return from Asia, he had
spent over a year in military hospitals until medication
had been discovered that would allow him to lead a
normal life. But without the daily medication were
periods of delirium, or more frightening, being
completely unable to communicate.

'You saw that,' he told her, 'the night you found me.
There was a time when I could see, and hear, and
understand you but I couldn't speak to you or let you
know I understood.' At Carolyn's horrified look, for
she was remembering all that she had said when she had
thought he was delirious, he laughed aloud, something
he did often now.

'You weren't the only one,' he consoled her. 'At first,
the doctors were always saying things they wouldn't
have said otherwise until they discovered what was
happening.' He paused thoughtfully. 'Most of them
thought I didn't have a chance in hell of surviving. I
proved them wrong.' Again a long pause.

'You're right, though. It isn't funny and I can't begin
to describe for you how horrible the feeling is. It's like
. . . it's like being accidentally locked in the prison of
your own body and nobody knows you're in there no
matter how hard you try to tell them.'

'But with the medication, this never happens to you, does it?'

'That's just it. To lead a normal life, I'm tied to a bottle of little white tablets. I'll never be completely free, the doctors say. However, they didn't think I would live, either. I wonder, sometimes, what would happen if I stopped taking them. It could be that after so much time has elapsed I will build up a resistance to the fever. It just needs to be conquered.'

Carolyn's answer was tart. 'It didn't look like that a couple of weeks ago. What is so terrible about being dependent on little pills. You are dependent on air, aren't you, and I don't hear you putting forth the possibility of holding your breath to see if you can do without it.'

Mike let out a great shout of laughter that shattered the morning stillness, causing a rabbit that had been hopping leisurely through the clearing to make a hurried run for cover. 'Lady, you're priceless,' he sputtered. 'You ought to have that tongue of yours registered as a deadly weapon. I've never seen anyone with such a steady ego-destroying aim. I surrender.' He raised his arms over his head and, still laughing, walked toward the cabin door to start breakfast, Carolyn's rueful laughter following him.

Though Carolyn and Mike could talk and laugh together in the daylight, they never touched—not the barest meeting of fingertips, not the most casual brushing of shirt sleeves. It was as if each knew that touching would break the delicate fragility of their relationship and it would be forever beyond mending.

In the night, however, they were enemies and lovers, though not in the sexual sense.

Michael continued to impose the good night kiss upon them, a ritual Carolyn dreaded, as, she was sure, did Mike. But Michael stood by in smug satisfaction as Carolyn brushed Mike's cheek with icy lips before she retired each evening. Her son seemed unaware that Mike's hands were clinched into rigid fists when she did so.

Every night, some time in the early morning hours, she went to Mike who still dreamed his part in past horrors. Now she was free to touch, to whisper soothing love words, to ease his troubled spirit into a more peaceful sleep or, as often happened now, gentle wakefulness. At such times, they never spoke and she never stayed, but he would gently squeeze her hand and give her his slow, sweet smile. His eyes would soften and beckon her into his soul and she would kiss them shut with warm, soft lips before rising and hurrying on trembling legs to her own bedroom to lie awake and restless until the smell of freshly made coffee once more re-established the rules of the day.

A pencil in her mouth and her list in her hand, Carolyn stood on tiptoe to check the contents of the kitchen cabinets one last time. Tomorrow morning they were leaving and she was making a list of supplies they would need to bring next time. She kept her mind firmly on the task at hand, determined to give no thought to tomorrow, or the next day, or any day in the future. A future without Mike in it was unthinkable and yet Mike had made no mention of seeing them after they left the mountain.

Michael, also, had been oddly silent on the subject and Carolyn sighed noisily through her pencil. Knowing she was being a coward didn't help when she wasn't sure she had what it took to broach the subject to her son herself.

'You sound like a horse blowing off flies,' said a deep

voice behind her and Carolyn whirled around, bumping her head on an open cabinet door.

Mike grimaced with her in sympathy, but he didn't touch her as she rubbed the side of her head. 'Careful,' he said mildly, if a trifle late.

'You startled me,' she said accusingly, taking the pencil from her mouth. Then she grinned. 'I almost bit my pencil in two.'

'Shouldn't have had it in your mouth—bad for the teeth,' he retorted. 'What I'm here for is to see if you would like to go riding. It is too pretty a day to be stuck inside. How about you, too, Mikie?' He turned to the boy sitting at the table, a wood carving and knife in his hands.

Carolyn was taking her hat and jacket from the peg and turned with some surprise when Michael answered, 'Not me, thanks, Sarge. I want to finish this before tomorrow.' 'This' was a small carving of a squirrel sitting on a tree branch. The surprise for Carolyn was that he had actually spoken of tomorrow. He seemed to have his attention fixed on the carving in his hand, so Carolyn couldn't read the expression in his eyes. Nevertheless, before walking out the door, she placed a hand on his shoulder. Still, he did not look at her and she walked into the cool, crisp sunshine, frowning.

Neither she nor Mike spoke as each saddled his horse and mounted. It was a companionable silence, however, that lasted until they rode across the meadow away from the cabin. They had often ridden together, sometimes alone, sometimes with Michael, and had found as much sharing in the silences as in the conversations.

Today the mountain didn't ease the worry for her son that preyed on Carolyn's mind. For once, it didn't offer a solution.

'What is it, Carolyn?'

'I'm worried about Michael. The thought of leaving you is hurting him and I don't know what to do about it or even how to handle it.' The words came without conscious thought and Carolyn found herself surprised at her directness. In her worry she hadn't thought before she spoke and now she was sorry! The problem was her own to handle and should not have been dumped on Mike. It would only make him feel guilty or uncomfortable.

As if to confirm her thoughts, Mike took off his hat and rubbed his arm across his forehead. He might have been removing perspiration but there was a breeze that carried the feel of the snow that was not far above them. He replaced the hat carefully and pulled it down low. When he spoke his tone was carefully without emotion. 'I know. I've known for the last few days it was bothering him. I guess I just didn't want to face it. I'll talk to him.'

Glancing at him, Carolyn saw a muscle leap in his jaw, as though his teeth were tightly clenched. Abruptly, she reined in her horse, surprising Mike into doing likewise.

He looked at her inquiringly and Carolyn blurted out, 'This isn't your problem, Mike. You didn't ask for any of this and you don't have to talk to him. I'll take care of it.'

The man sat easily on his horse, his arms crossed on the saddle horn. His hat shadowed his eyes but there was no mistaking the grin that split his face. He cocked his head to one side, pushed his hat back to reveal twinkling brown eyes, and said quite gently but with obvious relish, 'But-out, lady!'

Before she could open her mouth for an indignant reply, Mike held up one large hand as though stopping traffic. 'Carolyn, the relationship involved in this problem is between Mikie and myself. You have nothing to do with it. In your own words, Mother Wisdom, this is *none of your business!*' His grin could not have been more devilish.

Carolyn had to laugh. She had just been very neatly out-wisdomed. 'Oh, all right. I yield to greater truth. But you didn't have to enjoy it so much!'

Mike laughed softly with her for a moment before he promised quite seriously. 'I'll give him something he can live with. He's dear to me, too, you know.' He urged his horse forward so that his face was out of her range of vision.

Though Mike had really said very little, Carolyn felt much better. Her spirits lifting, she was able to enjoy their ride and to silently make her farewells to her favourite spots on the mountain. The man beside her did not intrude but followed wherever she led as if he understood that the mountain was a very old and dear friend whose faithfulness could be counted on in happiness and in sorrow. Perhaps Mike felt the same for the quality of the silence in their ride brought them a closeness that had never been expressed in the daylight hours.

Over an hour later, they were once more at the meadow. Across it they could see the cabin, a trickle of smoke coming from its chimney to dissipate in the thin mountain air. Carolyn was thinking what a peaceful scene it made, like something on an advertisement for mountain property, when smoke began billowing out of the cabin doorway. They always left the door closed when using the fireplace, she thought stupidly.

Beside her, Mike's horse leaped forward and hers was only a moment behind. Then she saw the bear come waddling hurriedly out of the cabin and before her horrified mind could take it in, the bear stood on its

back legs, waving its paws menacingly at their
approach. Carolyn's heart stopped, but Mike was
racing forward like one demented, yelling at the top of
his lungs. Carolyn could only do the same, though her
screams were close to hysterical. The bear dropped to
all fours and waddled with amazing speed in the
opposite direction.

She had leaped from her horse almost before it
stopped and was running for the cabin door when Mike
grabbed her, spinning her around.

'Stay here, Carolyn,' he said urgently. 'I'll go.'

'Michael! Michael's in there,' she sobbed, trying
without success to pull out of his grip.

He shook her briefly and hard, causing her hat to
come off and her hair to fly around her face. 'There is
fire in there, lady. You stay here ready to take care of
him. I'll bring him out.' He gave her one more little
shake, his hands gripping her shoulders, his eyes
burning into hers, willing her to obey. 'Do you
understand me?' She gave a small nod and he said more
gently, 'I'll go get him.'

But when Mike went through the door of the cabin,
his commands went with him. Carolyn didn't hesitate,
but was through the door after him to be met by a wall
of smoke. 'Michael!' she called and began coughing.
She could hear Mike, coughing also, but she could see
nothing but smoke, tears running down her cheeks as it
burned her eyes.

'Michael!' she gasped, but it was little more than a
whisper.

'Lie down on the floor, Carolyn.' Mike's voice, too,
was gasping. 'Get away from the door. I'm coming
through but I don't have Mikie.' She dropped to the
floor and immediately found it easier to breathe. She
found that she could see more also.

She saw Mike's big boots hurry past her and out the cabin door and miraculously, the smoke began to clear. She stood at once, going further into the room. 'Michael!' she called again frantically.

'I'm right here, Mom.' She whirled round to see him coming in the cabin door behind her. He ran to her and she clung to him, holding him tightly, her eyes closed, saying nothing, too overcome to express the joy she felt in holding him in her arms.

When at last she was able to let him go she held him away from her and examined him minutely but was thankfully unable to find any damage beyond a lingering fright still darkening his eyes.

The smoke was almost totally cleared from the cabin. Now able to look around her, she saw that it was in shambles. Chairs were overturned, as were the book shelves and occasional tables. Books and papers were scattered indiscriminately through the wreckage. Even the big kitchen table had been knocked over. Sugar and flour made a white drift over the floor, dirtied with coffee and grounds from the coffee pot. Shards of broken pottery added to the destruction and made walking hazardous. Amazingly, nothing was burned, though smoke stains covered everything.

However, strewn over the stone flooring in front of the fireplace were pieces of charred cloth and the stench of burned nylon permeated the cabin.

Carolyn, unable to take it all in, turned her back on it and hurried out the door in search of Mike. She found him stamping on the remains of Michael's rolled sleeping bag, testimony of what had been burning. 'Not much fire for so much smoke,' he said briefly but Carolyn stared at him in horror.

His eyes were red rimmed in a face grainy with smoke stain. But it was his shirt that held Carolyn's horrified attention. It's front was full of charred holes of varying sizes that had been burned into it as he had carried out the sleeping bag. Through some of them she could see his skin, red and raw. She looked at his hands but was relieved to see that he had been wearing riding gloves when he had picked up the burning cloth. However, one of them had a large hole burned into it along the base of the thumb.

'Michael,' she ordered briskly, 'there is still snow in places that get little sun. Find me some. Put on your jacket first,' she added when she realized he was still in his shirt sleeves. 'And Michael, hurry, please.'

'Sure thing, Mom,' and Michael raced into the cabin, coming out soon after in his jacket and carrying a large metal mixing bowl. As he ran around the side of the cabin, Carolyn called out, 'You look out for that bear!' He raised an arm in acknowledgement.

'Want to tell me what is going on?' asked Mike mildly.

She smiled. 'The best thing I know for a burn is cold. Snow, in this case, is quicker than ice.'

'Were you burned?' he asked, frowning as he turned her towards him and ran his eyes quickly over her body.

She stepped back quickly. 'Look at yourself, silly.' He looked down at himself, surprise on his face as he took in the holes in his shirt. 'You do look awful,' she added. 'Come and sit down on the bench. There is nowhere to sit inside and I need to put some snow on these burns. Where is your jacket, by the way?'

'Inside somewhere. I took it off thinking Mikie might need it.'

To cover the body, Carolyn thought grimly. She said nothing but something must have shown in her face for Mike said quickly, 'To use as a shield against fire, Carolyn.' He completely changed the subject by adding,

'You don't look so gorgeous yourself, you know.' When she gave a rather shaky smile he went on. 'I think your snow is wasted effort. I don't feel a thing. Probably only the shirt was burned.'

'You'll feel it as you warm up. Here is Michael. Take your shirt off.'

'That sounds like a proposition, lady,' he grinned as he unbuttoned the remains of his shirt, but he didn't look at her.

Michael came up to them just in time to hear his comment. 'What does that mean, Sarge?'

'Nothing,' Carolyn said hastily. 'Go into the cabin and bring Mike's other shirt, would you, please?'

With his shirt off, Mike's burns were easily seen. There were not as many as she had feared but there were three of fairly large size along his rib cage. As she held snow to them, her own hands also encased in leather riding gloves, she couldn't help but notice how the cold air made the scars around his neck and wrists stand out. She said nothing, keeping her eyes on her task. She knew if she looked up he would see the compassion in her eyes and hate it. Instead she said briskly, 'Dunk your thumb in the bowl of snow for a few minutes and that should do it. Not too long, though. You don't want frostbite.'

She wound a light layer of gauze around the burns on his ribs and did the same for the burn at the base of his thumb. Mike stood shrugging into his shirt, as Michael told them of his encounter with the bear.

It seemed that he had heard his horse acting up in the barn and had gone to check but could find nothing wrong. When he came back into the cabin he apparently didn't fasten the door securely; when he looked up, Old Joe was coming through it. 'When he came through that door I ran for the bathroom and slammed the door. I was really scared!'

He stayed in the bathroom listening to the bear as it foraged through the cabin. He had heard Mike and Carolyn coming but by that time wisps of smoke were coming in under the bathroom door. He called out, he said, but they didn't hear him. At that point he had opened and crawled out of the bathroom window, not daring to open the door.

During his recital, Carolyn rigidly kept her mind on his actual words, not the pictures of what might have been that her imagination insisted on conjuring. It was over, after all, and going to pieces would serve no purpose.

'Well, the cabin isn't going to clean itself,' was all she had to say when he finished. 'The sooner we start, the quicker we'll be finished,' and she went inside.

CHAPTER EIGHT

'MIKIE, would you see to the horses for me?' Mike asked gently. 'I think your mother is going to need some help.' Not waiting for a reply he stared for the cabin after Carolyn.

What he found was more or less what he had expected. She was standing in the kitchen area looking blankly at the flour scattered over the floor, the handle of a broken coffee mug in one hand, shaking uncontrollably, tears streaming unchecked down her face. Coming up to her unnoticed, Mike gently took the broken piece of pottery from her unresisting fingers and placed it on the draining board. Then just as gently he wrapped his arms around her. She turned into his shoulder as if she belonged there, sobbing her shock and fright into his broad, accommodating chest.

He held her trembling body close, smoothing her hair, saying nothing, knowing that words would have no meaning at this point. Gradually the wild sobbing eased, becoming small hiccups, and then small sniffles. Carolyn, to her shame, always cried like a child cries, with little grace and almost no dignity.

Mike held her a little away from him, looking down into her face to ask softly, 'Better?'

She nodded, giving him a watery smile. 'Your shirt is all wet.'

He, too, gave a small smile. 'It will dry,' and he pulled her back into his arms, resting his chin on the top of her head.

She lay there, listening to the steady drum of his

heart, feeling more safe and secure than she had in years. 'Oh, Mike, I do love you!'

She heard the whispered words in shock. Had she really said them aloud? By his instantaneous reaction, she knew she had.

Thrust from his arms as if she was unclean, she found herself staring into the face of a stranger. Eyes like brown stones in a face devoid of colour, his lips drawn back from his teeth to snarl like a wild thing, 'Shut up! Just shut-up!' His words were rasped slowly and distinctly, with a deadly edge.

But Carolyn had been suppressing her emotions for three weeks in a situation that had not been clear from the beginning. Her emotions all ready at peak, she was ready to do battle for their right to be. The words had been spoken and nothing could undo them. Now. Now she would face whatever it was what must be faced.

'Why, Mike?' she asked softly. 'Why should I shut up? You know there is something between us. Why must we never talk about it—or treat it as if it doesn't exist?'

His answer was unequivocal and cruel. 'Because, Carolyn, it doesn't exist, except in your imagination. My god, if you're so hot for a man why didn't you take your friend up on his offer? Why pick on me? Or do you just like a man to be helpless on occasion so you can get your kicks playing ministering angel?'

Carolyn felt his words like blows against her heart, against her self respect . . . and he hadn't finished.

Hands thrust into back pockets as though to keep from hitting her, he leaned forward slightly to make his final point. 'Don't you understand? You can not ever be a part of my life!'

She stood quite still as his words bombarded her, her eyes never leaving his face, mesmerised by the weapon

that was destroying her, a part of her mind noticing
how his skin was pulled tight across his cheekbones and
cords in the muscles of his neck quivered from his rigid
stance. She had gone beyond pain, or even anger, into
the numb no-man's-land of emotionless shock. She
waited a second to see if he was finished before saying
with what only she knew was a fake quietness, 'You
make yourself quite clear. I'm sorry if I've embarrassed
you. Now would you mind picking up the heavier
furniture while I start cleaning some of this mess?'

In spite of her words, neither of them moved. For
one long moment they stared at each other across an
endless gulf that neither was willing to span.

'Right,' said Michael at last, tiredly, and bent to
restore the kitchen table to its former position. Carolyn
saw his thumb rub over David's initials carved in small
letters on the under corner of the table before she, too,
turned to pick up the broom and began sweeping the
debris.

When Michael came in they were both hard at work
and the fact that they spoke little, if at all, went
unnoticed or at least unremarked.

Supper that night was tinned soup. They all ate with
little appetite and no enjoyment. Even Michael was
unusually silent. There were no jokes. Carolyn offered
to wash dishes alone as Mike and Michael played a last
chess game in front of the fire.

With the last dish in place she sat down at the kitchen
table to add to her list some now necessary items. It was
stained and spattered with coffee grounds from where
she had found it on the floor and was mute testimony
of the day's events. Carolyn was too dispirited to
recopy it. Looking down she saw that she had written
'courage' instead of coffee and gave herself a wry smile.
How blatantly Freudian could one be!

Michael came to ask if he could make some hot cocoa and Carolyn took the opportunity to rise from the table and say something vague about a headache. 'Just fix some for you and Mike. I think I'll have an early night. You need to be getting to bed pretty soon yourself. Remember, we have to leave before sun-up in the morning.' She kissed him and gave him a fierce hug that was returned with unusual vigour.

'Use my sleeping bag tonight,' she added, brushing his hair back from his forehead. 'It's in the storage closet. Goodnight, honey. Goodnight,' she said in Mike's general direction. Thank goodness she had sidestepped having to kiss him. She thought he wasn't going to answer and she was at the bedroom door before he made a quiet response.

'Goodnight.' It sounded softly final and she made no acknowledgment of hearing it, but her heart was pounding madly as she walked through the bedroom door.

In the bedroom she began removing her clothing, an article at a time, until she stood before her mirror in panties and bra. Gazing at herself a moment she then removed her bra and stepped out of her panties and then looked at herself again in the dim light of the lantern. Her legs were too long, as was her nose. Her breasts were too small and she was skinny. Her hair was too long to be short and too short to be long and it was the wrong colour. Her mouth was too wide and her ears stuck out and there were small stretch marks on her abdomen. She looked at herself with loathing before putting on a lopsided smile that didn't reach her eyes.

'You stupid lady,' she whispered to herself. 'If he loved you two heads wouldn't make any difference. Now behave yourself!' She stepped into a clean pair of panties and pulled a granny gown on over her head so that she was enveloped from head to toe. Giving herself a wink that she didn't believe in, she turned out the lantern and crawled into bed. For once, her dirty clothes were left where they lay and her face and teeth were unwashed.

She welcomed the total darkness of the room, loving the feel of its blackness against her open eyes, finding herself resenting the chink of light coming under the bedroom door. After a while it, too, was gone and she lay listening to the silence of the cabin, occasionally punctuated by the creak of settling wood or the distant hoot of an owl. A lump of misery existed where her heart should be but she didn't think and she didn't cry.

She knew that tomorrow would come and today would be forever in the past. This numb feeling of nothingness was not something new in her life but how horribly unfair it seemed to have to go through it twice!

She lay in bed through the night, not restless, actually moving very little. If Mike dreamed in the night she didn't hear him and she had left the door to her bedroom closed. When the bedside clock told her it was close enough to dawn, she got up, dressed for the ride down the mountain and stripped the bed. These sheets she would take with her, bringing clean ones the next time. For the first time she found no joy at the thought of ever returning to the cabin.

Emerging from the bathroom into the still dark cabin, Carolyn went into the kitchen area, lit the lantern and put the coffee on, shivering slightly in the chill. She lit the kerosene heater to give a little warmth so that they wouldn't have to use the fireplace.

She was frying bacon when she heard Mike go into the bathroom, and sighed quietly in relief. She had been afraid that she would have to wake him and wasn't sure she could have stood being so close to him.

They were all quiet on this last morning but much of Michael's tension seemed to have drained out of him. His quietness seemed more due to the early morning hour than anything else. Carolyn concluded that Mike had kept his promise to talk to him about their separation and was grateful for that, at least.

Before they began the journey down the mountain, Mike boarded up the cabin against the possibility of the return of Old Joe. As Mike drove in the final nails, Carolyn felt like there was a symbolism there somewhere. The cabin had never before denied entry to anyone and now, to get back in, she would have to tear the boards down. She kept her thoughts to herself and sat impassively on her horse, watching. Then Mike, too, mounted and they rode down the mountain to the valley below.

In the weeks that followed her return to Boulder, Carolyn often looked back upon her descent from the mountain with a sense of unreality. If her physical body had not come to be in her familiar apartment she would have been tempted to believe she had dreamed the transition from tranquil mountain to bustling, sophisticated city.

She had few memories of her trip down the mountain. Little had been allowed to penetrate her carefully blank mind—the creak of the saddles, the muffled footfalls of the horses on forest paths, Mike's broad shoulders as they swayed with the movement of his horse, the no-nonsense way he wore his stained and battered hat. Mike, of course, had led the way and because of the nature of the trail, they had ridden mainly single file, with Carolyn more often than not bringing up the rear. Conversation had of necessity been brief, if at all, for which she had been profoundly grateful. She had nothing to say to anyone and had been relieved not to be forced into trivialities.

Her mind had been a blank, self-protection against useless tears. She had thought no further ahead than the next break in the trees, the next bend in the trail. The mountain had presented her with its most glorious springtime beauty as a farewell gesture but her heart had refused to acknowledge the beauties that her eyes had blindly seen.

What she had said at parting at the Richardson's ranch where the horses were quartered she did not know. She remembered smiling. She and Michael had turned their horses into the Richardson's corral and they had all three been invited into the couple's cheery ranch kitchen for coffee and homemade doughnuts. Carolyn recalled vaguely something about a daughter's wedding in the conversation and she felt sure the price of hay had been discussed. It usually was.

But if conversation in the kitchen was a nebulous memory, she recalled with horror the feel of those doughnuts in her stomach as she had driven her ancient station wagon down the dirt ranch road to the highway. As soon as she was out of sight by the ranch she had pulled over to the side of the road and been sick. She had told Michael that she had just eaten too many of a good thing. Actually, she didn't think she would ever be able to eat a doughnut again as long as she lived. Even the smell now made her nauseous.

Once back at the apartment, however, her sense of unreality had vanished. Surrounded by city conveniences, the responsibility of being a student, teacher, and mother combined with the daily necessity of living by the clock served to make her feel that the weeks on the mountain had been a dream—a wonderful, heartbreaking dream, the sharp memory of which was with her every waking moment.

Michael, though subdued on the trip down the mountain, had recovered by the next day and once back in school was his old self. He talked about Mike on occasion but not excessively so, and Carolyn found her fears in that area lessening.

Carolyn studied assiduously for her own exams, took them, and to her surprise, did well. As an instructor she had also to prepare exams for her own students as well as grade them. Before she knew it the school term was almost over and summer vacation was just around the corner.

She had seen Steven on several occasions since her return and could see clearly now that though they could never be lovers she would never find a better friend. The mountain had taught her that.

Steven, for his part, seemed to sense the complete withdrawal of sexuality from their relationship and let it stay that way with no apparent surprise or hurt feelings. He called as often, took Michael on outings as often, and generally made himself useful as only a good male friend can. But his kisses were on the cheek, his hugs bearlike, and his hand on her elbow protective. Carolyn wondered a hundred times why her love for him never went beyond that of friendship. She didn't know a finer person.

One Saturday morning, a week before school was over for the summer for Michael, though Carolyn was already finished, she was in the kitchen preparing a tuna salad for their lunch when Steven came in, wiping greasy hands on an old rag.

'You now have a new clutch in that old heap, Carolyn. I'd say it if it had a new body you could call it a new car. There aren't many parts in it I haven't replaced this year. When you are going to break down and get a new one? You might as well, you know. It gets rather expensive buying one piece by piece.'

'I know,' Carolyn sighed, 'but I really like the old girl. She's comfortable and I never have to feel guilty about getting her dirty. All the same, it's not really fair taking so many of your weekends putting her back together.'

'You don't have to worry about that,' Steven grinned. 'It's always a challenge restoring an antique.'

'Mom, have you seen my red sweatshirt?' Michael's voice drifted in from his bedroom.

'It's in the drier,' Carolyn called back and then mused aloud, 'What could he want with his sweatshirt on a hot day like this?'

'I have all my stuff ready but that,' Michael said coming into the kitchen. 'Umm, tuna! May I have one of the dill pickles? I'm starving!'

'Help yourself. We can't have you collapsing on my clean kitchen floor.'

As Michael used a fork to spear a pickle from the jar, Carolyn asked in puzzlement, 'What stuff ready for what?'

'My gear to go camping, Mom. Don't you remember? The Sarge is picking me up at one o'clock this afternoon for an overnight fishing trip. We're camping out.'

Carolyn's face lost all its colour and she turned blindly towards the sink for a drink of water to hide her reaction from Michael until she could get her face under control. She opened the cabinet door and got herself a glass, her back to her son as he teased her, unaware of the havoc he had set into motion.

'You've been working too hard, Mom, or old age is catching up to you. Don't you remember? Sarge and I set up the trip coming down the mountain. This was the earliest day he could make it. He called the other day and gave me the time.' Michael stopped suddenly in his narration. 'Uh oh, I forgot to tell you that part. You were in class when he called and I had a Scout meeting that afternoon and I just forgot all about it. Guess old age is catching up to *me*!'

Carolyn had turned around by this time and could talk naturally though she clutched her glass of water for dear life. 'Well, Grandpa, the drier should be stopped by now. You can get your sweatshirt. Take the rest of the clothes out, too, and put them on my bed so I can fold them later. Wash your hands first,' she called as Michael went through the door.

'I need to do that myself,' Steven said ruefully, looking at his greasy hands. 'I'm assuming some of that tuna is for me?' he asked with the familiarity of an old friend.

'You know it is,' she smiled. 'I can't let you go hungry when you've just put the old girl back together!'

As soon as Steven left the room Carolyn sank into a kitchen chair, her trembling legs refusing to support her any longer. Mike was coming here! She couldn't take it in. She hadn't known he was even aware of where they lived. Somehow, she couldn't associate him with any place but the mountain, even knowing he was a wealthy business man.

But he wasn't a business man any longer. He had sold out his interests before coming to the mountain. So what was he doing now? Where had he gone when they had left the mountain? Where was home?

Questions skittered around Carolyn's mind like squirrels—questions she had never thought to ask. On the mountain nothing had existed for her but the preciousness of each day. She had confronted the horrors of Mike's past but had never confronted the future. When they had left the mountain, she had somehow thought they would never see each other again. And now he was here; would be here in just an hour!

She sprang out of her chair to stand indecisively, her mind in a whirl over what to do first—straighten the living room or take a fast bath? She was hurrying towards the kitchen door when she stopped in midstep and laughed aloud at her own foolishness before going back to the table where she had been preparing lunch.

The first thing you are going to do, lady, she chided herself, unconsciously using Mike's word for her, is get yourself under control and stop acting like a lovesick teenager. Then you are going to finish making a tuna salad and feed it to the hungry people in this apartment. *If* there is time you can look over the living room and see if there is any obvious mess and then you *might* brush your hair out of this pony tail. You will remember, she told herself sternly, chopping pickles with vigour, that he is only coming to pick up your son, not to visit you. He will probably not be in the living room longer than five minutes.

Carolyn was very good about following her own advice, though at lunch she ate little and had to be told to pass the salt twice. Her colour was high, her eyes sparkled and in her jeans and T-shirt she looked very like the teenager she was trying so hard not to emulate. For a fleeting moment wistfulness showed itself clearly in Steven's eyes before his face once more organised itself into its usual look of friendly cheerfulness.

Ordinarily, he would have left after lunch but he said something about a final adjustment that needed to be made on the car and went out. He had just finished cleaning his hands again and was in the living room when the doorbell rang.

Carolyn was in her bedroom running a brush through her hair and to her the musical chimes sounded like a death knell. Her hands trembling, she deliberately put the brush back on the dresser, straight up and down and just so, before going to answer the door.

She was half way across the living room, however, when Michael came running from his room, threw the door open and himself into Mike's arms. 'Golly, Sarge, I've missed you!' the boy said exuberantly into the big man's belt buckle.

'I've missed you, too, Mikie,' came the familiar deep rumbling tones but Carolyn couldn't see his face, only the top of his crisply curling hair as he bent over her son. She felt her heart give a squeeze as the warmth and love in their greeting seemed to permeate the room.

When at last he looked up, she had her face under control and was able to greet him with calm serenity, extending her hand in greeting, and saying without a trace of a tremble, 'Hello, Mike.' The warmth of his clasp sent her heart knocking but only by a small flicker of an eyelash did she show it.

Mike's face and eyes were as bland as her own and if he held her hand a moment longer than necessary, it was probably because he was momentarily distracted by Michael, who said admiringly, 'Wow, Sarge! You look super!'

For the first time Carolyn noticed his apparel and caught her breath. He was wearing a light grey business suit that had the suggestion of a western cut, emphasising his broad shoulders and lean hips. From the top of his hand-stitched boots to his expertly barbered hair he looked what all the newspaper gossip

columnists said he was—a very successful, very sexy
business man and entrepreneur.

Carolyn felt a shock run through her. She didn't
know this man! In this setting and in a business suit he
was a total stranger. Slowly, she relaxed. She could deal
with a stranger. It was the man of the mountain that
caused her heart and her instincts to go crazy. 'You
certainly look very distinguished, Mike,' she smiled—a
polite smile, the kind she kept for meeting strangers for
the first time. Mike lifted an eyebrow.

'Thanks,' he said, ruffling Michael's hair. 'I'm just off
a plane and thought I'd better come straight on here
since I'm running a bit late. If it's all right with you,
Mikie, I'd like to use your bedroom to change into
something more suited to fishing before we go.'

'Sure, Sarge. C'mon, I'll show you my room.'

'Michael,' his mother remonstrated, 'if Mike is just
off a plane perhaps he would like to relax a few minutes
first.' She looked inquiringly at Mike, completely at
ease and able to act the good hostess now that her mind
had safely put this man behind a shield of strangeness.
'Won't you sit down for a while?' she suggested. 'I've
just made a fresh pot of coffee, or perhaps you would
rather have a beer?'

But Mike was looking over her shoulder, his face
now hard as granite. She turned to see what had caught
his attention and suddenly remembered Steven, who
had remained in the living room when she had
answered the door.

Steven, smiling, came forward, lean and graceful in
his grubby jeans and grease stained T-shirt, not at all
embarrassed by his own attire. 'Hello, Mike. I've heard
a great deal about you. I'm Steven Ramsey,' and he
thrust out his hand.

'I believe I've heard the name,' said Mike, irony

weighting his voice, returning the handshake. Both men were smiling but their eyes were guarded and wary. The handshake was brief and hard.

'If you don't mind, Carolyn, I'd rather get out of this suit before having some of that coffee. Mikie, would you help me bring in my bag?'

When they had left, Steven, too, said he needed to be leaving. 'Oh, can't you stay a little longer? Have coffee with us!' Carolyn asked, not realising how beseeching was her tone of voice.

'Wouldn't you rather see him alone?' Steven asked gently. 'After all, it has been a long time.'

She flushed slightly, a little self-conscious at his perception, but said steadily, 'No, I don't really want to see him alone. I would appreciate your staying.' Steven looked at her intently before silently nodding his head. Impulsively Carolyn put her hand on his arm. 'You're a good friend, Steven.'

'I know,' he said with mock ruefulness, giving her a crooked grin that only partially covered an underlying seriousness.

Carolyn's hand was still on his arm when Mike and Michael came back into the apartment, Michael carrying a small valise and Mike with an empty suit bag over his shoulder. Mike's eyes narrowed as he glanced at them but he only said briefly, 'Coming through,' and gave a curt nod in Steven's general direction before following Michael to his bedroom.

Flustered, Carolyn, too, hurried to leave the room. 'I'd better make the coffee.'

She was at the kitchen door when Steven called her name. She turned to find him laughing at her across the room. 'It's all ready made,' he said in a stage whisper. She stood absolutely still for a moment before her laughter joined his.

'Oh, Steven,' she said, half laughing, half serious. 'I never realised I had it in me to be such a big fool!'

'Never that, Carolyn,' he said, the laughter sliding from his face at once. 'Never that.'

'Thank-you,' she said quietly and then smiled, 'I'll get the tray ready.'

'Now that sounds reasonable,' he smiled at her.

In the kitchen, Carolyn put cups and saucers on the tray and added a plate of chocolate chip cookies she had made that morning. Looking at the pretty cups, she couldn't help but think of pottery mugs and chilly sunrises on the mountain. Carefully, she allowed her mind to go no farther, but picking up the tray, made her way back into the living room where she could hear the men's voices.

Keeping a careful eye on the heavy tray, she didn't really look up until she neared the sofa and then almost dropped it! Sitting there, at his ease, was not the suave businessman-stranger that had arrived. This was the Mike her heart knew intimately, whose combination of strength and vulnerability played on the strings of her soul. This was the man she couldn't help but love and who had rejected that love in no uncertain terms. In jeans and knitted shirt, open at the throat, his size and masculinity seemed to dominate the room. Only Steven's own brand of cool maleness kept him from being overshadowed. With shaking hands, her heart drumming in her breast, she set the tray on the coffee table.

She didn't want to look at him, but against her will and instincts, her eyes rose to his face. He was smiling derisively as she had known he would be, his eyes mocking as she had known they would be—but she hadn't expected a twinkle behind the mockery nor the velvet warmth behind the twinkle that made her insides flip over and drop to her knees.

How dare he sit there like a pasha laughing at her! How dare he when he didn't love her! Carolyn wasn't quite sure of the logic behind her anger but she wasn't in the mood to be logical. She glared at him. Mike's grin broadened and one eyebrow lifted interrogatively, but his eyes grew wary. Turning on her heel, Carolyn headed back towards the kitchen, muttering, 'I forgot the sugar.'

'You certainly did!' There was a distinct laugh in Steven's voice as it just barely reached her across the room. Mike's answering chuckle echoed agreement. Men!

The two men and Michael were deep in a discussion of fly-tying techniques when she returned and she found herself superfluous to the conversation since fishing had never been one of her pleasures. From there it went on to favourite fishing holes and inevitably, to the ones that got away. No one touched the sugar.

Carolyn listened, allowing the talk to flow around her, lapping against her eardrums, soothing her with its friendly currents. She watched the two men as their hands punctuated their conversation. Her mind contrasted, compared, found neither man wanting, and she wondered once again why her heart couldn't find its home with Steven, who was a fine, good man and whose only short-coming seemed to be that he wasn't Mike.

Each man had so much to offer in looks, manners, and life-style. Each had that mysterious something that acted as a magnet to women. Steven's looks and bearing were those of a greyhound, long, lean, and powerful. In contrast, Mike was like a great dane; massive, but with an unique grace of his own.

Carolyn, deep in her thoughts, was slightly confused when the men stood up. Quickly she stood also. She must have looked her confusion for Mike informed her that he and Michael were leaving now since they had quite a drive ahead of them. His tone of voice implied that he was repeating himself.

'It's been a long time since I've had such an enjoyable conversation, Steven,' he said sincerely. He shook the other man's hand. 'I'm glad to have met you.' He paused before adding, 'And I wish you well.' His tone held no special significance but Steven's eyes gleamed speculatively for a moment as he returned the handshake and added civilities of his own.

Mike turned to Carolyn. 'I'll have Mikie home about six tomorrow afternoon,' he told her, adding the name of the national park that was their destination. He put out his hand and Carolyn put hers into it. At her touch, a flame seemed to leap in his eyes and he pulled her towards him, giving her a brief, hard kiss on her surprised mouth. Before she could respond it was over. He threw Steven a half belligerent, half apologetic look, put on and pulled down low his battered, stained, and dearly familiar hat, and left the apartment.

In a daze, Carolyn hugged her son goodbye, too bewildered to give him the usual motherly admonishments. She didn't even notice that he left with a large, satisfied grin on his face.

CHAPTER NINE

CAROLYN stood staring at the closed door until Steven said softly, 'He's quite a man, your Mike.'

'Yes, he is,' she answered dreamily, before she could stop herself. The sound of her own words brought her back to reality and she whirled around, her eyes flying to Steven's face. He knew.

'I knew there was someone,' he said gently, in answer to her unspoken question, 'and I thought it might be the man you met over the Easter holidays. Now I know it for sure.

'Michael told me who he is and how you met,' he continued, 'and you know how great Michael thinks he is. After meeting him, I have to agree with Michael's opinion. To tell you the truth, I didn't think I would like him, but I do.'

He looked at her silently for several seconds, examining her face. 'You love him very much, don't you?'

The words were softly spoken but they tore her apart. Tears came unbidden, tears she had sworn she would not shed again. She didn't know how but she found herself sobbing into Steven's chest. His arms were around her holding her as if she were a weeping child as the pent up misery of the past weeks flooded over her. She cried, cried until there were no tears left and not once did Steven try to stop her.

When at last she lay quietly against him, all too well aware of the last time she had cried in a man's arms, he held her slightly away from him so that he could see her face, much as Mike had done. With one hand he wiped the dampness from her cheeks. 'Go wash your face now, honey, and we'll talk.'

Carolyn gave him a tremulous smile before doing as he told her. How words and actions seem to repeat themselves in different circumstances, she thought irrelevantly. When she returned, Steven had poured each of them a generous glass of brandy. She liked the taste of brandy in normal times and now she appreciated its fiery warmth as it seemed to burn away the last of the tears in her throat.

'All better?' Steven smiled.

'All better,' she affirmed, smiling back now with confidence.

'Want to talk?'

'There is really very little to say,' she said flatly. 'I love him. He doesn't love me. It's as simple as that.' She rubbed the rim of her glass with one finger, staring into its amber depths. So much pain in so short a statement.

'Funny, that wasn't my impression at all,' Steven answered her. When Carolyn looked at him inquiringly, he went on. 'Mike couldn't take his eyes off you, Carolyn. The whole time we were talking fishing he was watching you daydream. And another thing, when he and I were introduced I saw murder in his eyes and no mistake. I think he was jealous as hell over my being here.'

Though Carolyn put no faith in them, the words warmed her heart. She searched Steven's face, seeing nothing but sincerity. Taking a small sip of her drink, she said at last, sadly, 'As much as I would like to believe you, Steven, it just can't be so,' and she went on to tell him of Old Joe's entrance into the cabin and the events that had subsequently followed. Steven listened attentively, occasionally asking a question. When she had finished, she found herself holding her breath, waiting for his reply. Perhaps there was something that she had missed that would prove her wrong.

'I'm afraid it sounds pretty straightforward,' Steven confirmed disappointingly. At her sigh, he continued. 'But what you said of Mike's reaction and what I saw really don't match up. Are you sure you weren't so emotionally involved that you misunderstood what was said?'

Carolyn shook her head miserably. She knew that the words would be printed in her heart for as long as she lived.

'That being the case,' Steven said briskly, getting to his feet and reaching for her hand to pull her up with him, 'what is called for at this point is a change of scenery.' He looked her over with mock sternness. 'Get out of those jeans and into something frilly and feminine. I'm taking you to the swankiest restaurant a poor teacher can afford and then I have tickets to a rock concert. Nothing like a little screaming to the beat of a drum to help one to forget one's troubles,' he added pedantically. 'How does that sound?'

'Fun,' was Carolyn's succinct answer. She was not at all sure she wanted to go out but knew her only real reason for refusing would be a desire to brood.

'Right on,' he grinned, using the current vernacular. 'I look like something that just crawled out from under a car and it will take awhile to pretty me up. Also, I have a few errands to run. I'll be back in a couple of hours to collect you. Okay?'

'Okay,' Carolyn agreed. For a moment Steven gazed into her face, the smile sliding from his own as he touched her cheek with one finger. Carolyn looked back at him with equal seriousness and Steven could see a faint regret in her eyes. Both of them knew that any chance of a more intimate relationship had today drawn its last breath.

Suddenly, Steven was grinning again. 'I give you fair warning,' he said direly, 'I expect something sensational!'

With a trace of mischief, she answered his challenge, 'So do I!'

Carolyn, having earlier felt she would never smile again, had a wonderful time that evening.

True to her promise, she had pulled out all the stops when she had dressed so that the final result was one of outrageous chic.

Steven had given her enough time for a long, leisurely bubble bath with which she indulged herself, allowing the warm bubbles to pull the tension from her body and keeping her mind firmly fixed on what colour to paint her nails, both finger and toe. After taking her time with her bath, she dried herself and liberally applied the expensive talc that she used only on special occasions, before wandering naked into her bedroom to select her lingerie.

Looking it over she decided on panties only. She didn't want to wear a bra. She was feeling bold, and daring and sensual—and, she had to admit, defiant. Basically, she knew that under the expensive silky talc and the buff coloured scraps of her briefs, there was a consuming fear of the emptiness of the future for her without Mike. So tonight she would let her body dictate, not her head and definitely not her heart.

Sitting down at her dressing table, clad only in her briefs, she polished her nails with a pearly pink varnish and let her mind wander over her wardrobe, still undecided about what to wear. When her polish dried she applied her make-up with deft, sure strokes, using a greater variety than usual but with a light hand.

She stood back to look at the results—and stared. The person looking back at her, seemingly poised before the mirror for flight, bore little resemblance to her usual self. The iridescent green eyeshadow gave her eyes depth and a hint of mystery. Her shining cap of hair, swinging to her shoulders with a slight curl forward, emphasised her cheekbones and the tilt of her eyes. With her slim hips and small thrusting breasts, she looked like a woman who had just discovered sin—and enjoyed it. Female sexuality seemed to radiate from her. Carolyn suddenly felt herself blushing from her cheeks to her toes.

Hastily, she turned away from the mirror. I don't care, she thought rebelliously. I don't want to be me tonight. But as she once again looked over the clothes hanging in her closet a little niggling voice in a corner of her mind whispered. This is you, silly!

'Oh, go away!' she said peevishly and then grimaced. It's supposed to be all right to talk to yourself, she thought, but when you start answering yourself, you know you're in trouble! She giggled softly in the silent room.

Coming to a sudden decision, she pulled on a sheer white blouse with full sleeves gathered at the wrists. Then she added a pair of what were supposed to be pantaloons, flamingo pink with elastic gathers at the knee. However, instead of pulling them up to the knee, she allowed the gathers to remain at her ankles. Both of these articles of clothing had been portions of costumes for little theatre productions she had had parts in.

She rummaged in the bottom of her closet until she found a pair of high heeled sandals that consisted of little more than three black patent straps and a rhinestone buckle. She didn't often wear heels this high and they took her a while to locate. Without her customary hose her small bare feet in the strappy sandals took on a sensuality of their own.

Nerving herself before she went to the mirror, Carolyn surveyed her image once more. The pink pants gave her an all-over glow and the pink of her nipples seemed to push against the sheer material of her blouse. Carolyn added some long gold chains and some bangle bracelets and gazed at herself thoughtfully before shaking her head at her reflection.

It was no use. No matter how defiant she felt she knew she could never confront Steven with her breasts showing so blatantly. Yet a bra would be clearly seen through the material of the blouse and to change her blouse she would have to change her complete outfit. She had nothing else that she could wear with the pants.

To add to her dilemma, the door bell rang. Hurrying into the living room, she called through the door, 'Steven?'

'Here I am, ready or not!' he called back facetiously.

'Not,' Carolyn answered him. 'Give me a minute and then come in and fix yourself a drink. I won't be but a few more shakes.'

'This better be good,' he threatened as she unlocked the door, leaving it closed.

She said nothing, slightly pink cheeked. She couldn't think of a comeback that wasn't only too true at the moment. She scurried back to the bedroom, closing the door, and went to look yet again through the clothes hanging in her closet. Immediately her eyes fell on a peasant costume she had worn last year in a play. It had a long ruffled skirt, gaily trimmed in bands of ribbon, but best of all, it had a mint green satin bolero whose predominant trim was flamingo pink. Just the thing!

She pulled the bolero on over her blouse and checked herself yet again. Much better. She still looked sensual and exciting but the bolero covered her so that nothing was actually seen but everything was hinted. *Now* she felt wicked, but not quite like a streetwalker. She coated her lips with a pearl pink lipstick that gave them a moist, shiny look, dabbed some of the perfume that went with her talc behind her ears with a liberal finger, added some to the base of her throat, gave herself a last defiant look in the mirror and went to greet Steven.

'My god, Carolyn! You should get upset more often! You look sensational!'

'Those were my instructions,' she said with downcast eyes and mock demureness, and then completely lost her look of exotic mysteriousness with an impish grin. 'You look a bit sensational yourself,' she said, surveying him with lifted eyebrows.

He wore a black dinner jacket that fitted to perfection with a white shirt of some soft material that had ruffles down the front. He had not worn a tie but had left the shirt open at the throat, giving him an aura of indolent grace. 'Jaguar At Rest' Carolyn titled him in her mind. Without warning, she suddenly realised that as close as they were, she really didn't know Steven very well at all. She felt sure that there was much he had never let her see.

'One would think two such sensational people would make a sensational couple,' he said softly, as if reading her mind.

'So one would think,' returned Carolyn, striving for a light tone. She was suddenly cautious of where this conversation was headed.

'Which just goes to show the trouble one can get into by thinking,' Steven told her wickedly, knowing he had made her nervous for a moment and enjoying the fact. But he was serious when he added, 'I thought I was in love with you, Carolyn, until I saw you with Mike.

Somehow, when I compared emotions, it seemed as though mine were pretty shallow.' He touched her cheek lightly with a long, slim finger. 'I realise that what I thought was love is actually a very deep liking and respect—in short, friendship.' He smiled a crooked smile that found a place only on his lips, but Carolyn was too relieved to notice. 'Does that ease your mind?'

'Yes, it does,' was her honest reply. Carolyn, too, could now smile. 'Good friends can be just as important in one's life as lovers, Steven, and your friendship means a great deal to me.'

Steven held up the last of his drink. 'Here's to sensational friendships,' and if there was mild bitterness in his words it was swallowed with his drink. 'Now, ma'am, are you ready for the city lights?'

'Ready!' she laughed, and took his arm.

He took her to one of the city's better restaurants and nightspots which, at this early hour, was not as crowded as usual. Carolyn was pleased and surprised that her own clothes seemed in the mode of the other patrons. She noticed too, that several pairs of feminine eyes followed them as Steven led her to their table but she was unaware that several masculine ones showed marked interest in their progress, also.

Her dinner was superb and Steven a lively and witty partner. He treated her as if she was the most beautiful woman in the room, and the most fascinating, and Carolyn's badly bruised ego expanded a little, gently eased with cocktails before dinner and a bottle of wine with their meal. Coffee and liqueurs followed so that Carolyn was euphoric as they joined the throng pouring into the theatre for the rock concert.

She didn't mind that they were outstanding in their evening clothing in a crowd considerably younger than themselves and uniformly clad in tight jeans with every kind of top imaginable. Several of her former students were there and they greeted her and Steven with enthusiasm, complimenting them on their dress. She knew the compliments were, in their way, sincere but she smiled at the look on their faces that said the older generation was capable of anything. The boys, however, were definitely admiring and Carolyn found herself glad that classes were over for the term. She wasn't sure she could have faced them Monday morning.

Their ticket numbers put them near the front and situated so that they would receive the full effects of huge sets of speakers placed on either side of the stage. After they were seated, Carolyn asked curiously, 'Did you actually pay money for these tickets?'

'Actually, they were a gift from a student who couldn't make it,' Steven grinned. 'Don't you like Montage?' and he named the group that would be playing.

Carolyn wrinkled her forehead in thought. 'Never heard of them,' she said at last.

'My dear, you must start listening to the right radio stations if you are going to know how the other half lives,' was Steven's rejoinder as the crowd began cheering and a young man wearing puce satin pants, a white tee shirt with holes in it (Carolyn would have used it for dusting furniture), and no shoes ran out on to the stage. He yelled once at the audience and the audience, to Carolyn's surprise, yelled back. From then on the building reverberated with the heavy beat of drums, electric guitar, and organ.

The audience was wild, the performers were wilder, and everyone had a marvellous time. At one point, Carolyn turned to Steven and yelled, knowing that in the din only he would hear her, 'This is awful!'

'I know!' Steven yelled back. 'Great, isn't it?' and Carolyn laughed.

She was pleasantly exhausted after the concert and said as much, so that Steven, appearing not to mind in the least, took her back to the apartment. She invited him in for coffee and they were laughing as they went through her apartment door. Her laughter stopped abruptly, however, when she found all the lights on. Her heart pounding, she walked into the living room before Steven could stop her. Hearing a door open, Steven grabbed her and shoved her behind him.

Mike came into the room stopping as his eyes wandered over Carolyn, Steven's hand still gripping her arm, before saying coldly, 'You might hold the noise down. Mikie just fell asleep.'

All the colour drained from Carolyn's face and it was a second before she could speak. When she did her voice was high and shrill, not like her usual serene tones at all. 'What is it? Is Michael all right? What are you doing here?' Her questions tripped over themselves.

'Mikie developed a touch of stomach virus, is all,' answered Mike calmly. 'I thought it best to bring him back here. He had his key so I let us in and put him to bed. There was medication in the bathroom cabinet that he said you give him for this sort of thing.'

'Yes,' she murmured. 'He's had it before. It has gone around a couple of times this year.' Her voice was vague. It was an unpleasant feeling to have her child sick and not be here when he came in. It didn't help that Mike confirmed her feelings by looking at her as if she was the horrible mother she was thinking herself to be. 'Excuse me,' and she hurried into the bedroom to reassure herself that Michael was all right.

As Mike had said, he was asleep, looking soft and sweet as children do when asleep. She checked for fever, but there was none though his cheeks were pale and his mouth colourless. He would probably be up and sick again soon before the worst was over. She pulled the covers up over him more closely and turned to leave the room, to find Mike at the door watching her with flat, cold eyes. Her heart jumped up and, as he stood aside to silently let her pass, she wondered for the thousandth time why he seemed to dislike her so much.

In the living room she found Steven preparing to leave. 'I'll have that coffee another time,' he said quietly. 'Michael needs you now. Give him a hug for me.'

'I will,' answered Carolyn, going to the door with him. 'And, Steven, I had a wonderful time this evening. Thank-you for that.'

'My pleasure. Hang in there now,' he whispered significantly, and winked before letting himself out.

She turned back into the living room, a pensive look on her face, completely unprepared for what followed. 'Why so sad? Did a sick child interfere with a weekend with your lover?' Mike sneered.

'Of course not. I ...'

His voice slashed across her protests. 'Did you have a nice, quiet weekend in bed planned, maybe, with a few titillating games on the side?' He looked her up and down insultingly, his eyes not missing a thing.

'That's not fair!' she protested. 'We just went out, that's all. Steven is a friend...'

'Friend! Is that what they're called now?' He took no notice of her gasp of outrage, grabbing her wrist as she raised her hand to slap him. He looked down at her contemptuously to see her face filled with fury, eyes ablaze, her chest heaving. His own face was equally furious as his temper poured over her, but Carolyn was too angry to be frightened. She struggled to release her arm as he continued relentlessly. 'This is how you dress for your *friends*, is it?' His voice was a snarl and before she knew what he was about, he had ripped the little bolero off her. Surprise held her speechless for a moment as he gazed his fill at her body showing in misty outline through the sheer material of the blouse, a strange look on his face.

Carolyn felt the anger go out of her and a sudden rush of warmth take its place. The heat of it filled her face and she felt her nipples harden against the fabric of her blouse.

Mike's eyes, of course, missed nothing and travelled over her, from the pink aureoles of her thrusting breasts to the pulse hammering at her throat, before coming to rest on her warm, moist lips. 'Seems like any man will do,' he said thickly.

'You don't understand . . .' Carolyn tried to protest.

'You're right. I don't understand how a good man like David can be married to a two-timing woman like you,' Mike ground out as he pulled her roughly to him and covered her mouth with his own. His kiss was hard and demanding and Carolyn clamped her mouth closed against it, struggling to get free, hitting at his chest with her fists. She might as well have been a mosquito for his only response was to hold her so close that the only place her hands could reach were his broad shoulders. She reached higher to pull his head away from hers but somehow, instead her fingers became entangled in his curls.

The touch of his hair against her fingers was like a magic button that seemed to release all the love she had dammed inside of her. Her mind lost all control and her heart took over so that she leaned weakly against him, her mouth opening of its own volition under his. His kiss gentled and deepened and her whole being became centred on loving and being loved by Mike Flemming; on giving everything there was inside her to give to this big man to whom her heart, without her consent, had given itself. Her breasts swelled to his touch and throbbed beneath his gently questing fingers.

His hands on her body were gentle now as they explored its contours over and over, seemingly unable to get enough of the feel of her. He kissed her eyes, her throat, and, opening her blouse, her breasts. She stood quiescent under his hands, her head thrown back, drunk on his touch and smell. A warm, velvet feeling was invading her lower limbs and when he picked her up and carried her to the bedroom she hardly noticed.

He sat her on the side of the bed and took her sandals off, one by one, holding each small foot in his large hand and kissing her pink painted toes. Still kneeling, he trailed his fingers up her leg to her waist where he quickly unhooked her pants. When she was out of them, his tongue explored her bellybutton and Carolyn's hands were shaking as she reached to unbutton his shirt.

In bed beside her, he slowly continued removing her blouse, raining kisses of fire over her shoulders and breasts and stomach. Carolyn's hands, too, explored his body, loving the feel of it, claiming it for her own. At one point she covered his scars at neck and wrists with kisses, wishing her lips could remove them forever. Mike held her close to him for a moment when her lips went from his neck to his cheek and sighed deeply as though some part of him, deep inside, had been released, before once more arousing her to mindlessness.

Their lovemaking was everything Carolyn could have hoped it would be, except for one thing—Mike never spoke, never whispered love words as she did, never called her by name. It wasn't until they lay exhausted side by side that words Mike had spoken earlier rang warning bells in Carolyn's mind.

She was turning towards him to speak when his voice came hissing softly out of the darkness, to strike without warning, 'Poor Steven really missed it tonight.'

Quick as thought, Carolyn's closed fist struck him in the jaw and she was standing beside the bed shaking with fury. Her voice was cold and hard as his own could be as she said with measured menace, 'You listen to me, Mike Flemming. Steven is my *friend*, no more and certainly no less. You keep your dirty mouth off him! We are not lovers and never have been. My last lover was David.

'David is dead! You can't two-time the dead. We had a wonderful life together and loved each other very much. David was a giver, not a taker and he left me full of love, not empty. It's because he loved me so much that I can love again, freely and without guilt. It is what I would want for him if the situation was reversed. You certainly didn't know David very well if you didn't realise the kind of love he had for me was never meant to be a chain around my neck. Your filthy mind makes me sick!'

In the darkened room her proud naked body was pearlescent, but her quietly spoken words dropped like stones into the gloom. She couldn't see Mike in the darkness except the pale oval of his face and the blurred shapes of his arms and shoulders. He held himself curiously still as she continued, her words all the more incisive for being quietly spoken. 'Get out of my house, Mike Flemming. Get out of my life. If I never see you again it will be too soon.'

There was a slight movement from the bed but at that moment she heard Michael's voice, 'Mom?'

She grabbed up her bathrobe, wrapping it around her quickly before hurrying to the door. But before leaving the room she turned to the figure on the bed who still hadn't spoken and said two words clearly and distinctly, 'Go *now*.'

Michael was in the bathroom being sick again and she stayed with him, washing his face and giving him more of the medicine before putting him back to bed. She sat with him until he went back to sleep, hearing no sound from anywhere in the apartment, though she strained her ears. No thoughts formed, no hurt touched her, nor remorse.

At last she went back to her bedroom and standing at the door, switched on the light. The room was empty as she had expected it to be, only the tumbled sheets giving evidence that the bed had been used, the two pillows similarly indented. Carolyn went to the bed and sat down on the side of it. She sat very still for a long moment before reaching over and picking up the pillow Mike had used. Holding it to her face, she breathed in the scent of him before getting up and once more turning off the overhead light. Going back to the bed she lay down on top of it, regardless of tumbled sheets, her head on the pillow Mike had used, her feet tucked up under her bathrobe. She lay, staring dry-eyed into the darkness, until morning light filtered through the blinds and a new day began.

Michael's illness passed with the night in the way of such illnesses and at breakfast he declared himself 'starving!' Carolyn, however, limited his meal to scrambled eggs and toast, much to his disgust.

Leaving him to finish eating she was going through the living room to see if the Sunday paper had come when she saw the box. It lay on top of the coffee table and beside it was a folded note. Carolyn, drawn as if by a magnet, reached for the note, even as her eyes told her it was addressed to Michael. Knowing she shouldn't be reading it, she could no more stop her eyes from running over the brief message than she could have stopped breathing.

The note simply told Michael that he, Mike, had been called away and that it would be awhile before he could get in touch. The box, it said, contained a spare set of wood carving tools that Michael might enjoy using. It concluded with the simple sentence, 'Take care of your mother,' and was signed, 'Sarge.'

Her hands trembling, she replaced the note and as she did so, noticed that the 'spare set of tools' was the same ones that Mike had had with him on the mountain. He had taken meticulous care of them and Carolyn was certain that they meant a great deal to him. She knew that this was his way of saying goodbye to Michael and her throat flooded with tears, though her eyes remained dry.

Had she not considered Michael enough when she had told Mike to stay out of her life? Perhaps she had been selfish. On the other hand, she didn't think Michael could handle the now open conflict between her and Mike. No, it was better to leave things as they were. Somewhere, behind a closed door in her mind, the words, 'Poor Steven really missed it tonight' whispered nastily.

When she went back to the kitchen she told Michael of the box in the living room in a clear emotionless voice.

Michael was quite disappointed that he would not be seeing the Sarge but was thrilled with the gift. He, too, recognised the tools and realised how much faith Mike had in his ability to take care of them. He touched them reverently before going back to the note. 'He says I'm supposed to take care of you, Mom. Now why do you think he said that? I thought you were supposed to take care of *me*. I'm the one who was sick!'

'Maybe he means for us to take care of each other,' his mother answered gently giving his shoulders a squeeze.

'You know, Mom, I'll always take care of you if you need me.' His voice was young and very serious and Carolyn was touched to the heart of her. Then with a mercurial change of subject, as though afraid of getting too sentimental, he asked, 'Where were you last night, by the way?' and gave her a roguish look, comical on his freckle-dusted face.

Carolyn laughed. 'You'll never guess! Steven took me to a rock concert!'

'Wow! Who did you go see?' When Carolyn told him he was very impressed and laughed when she confessed to not knowing anything about the group. 'Mom, the best way to take care of you is to bring you up to date. You're hopelessly behind the times!'

'Believe me, Michael, there are times when ignorance is truly bliss,' she said drily and for the moment her problems were forgotten as she gave herself up to the enjoyment of conversation with her son. It wasn't until later that she wondered how and when Mike had left the box.

CHAPTER TEN

THE weeks passed and summer arrived in earnest, the heat enervating after the unusually harsh winter. Ordinarily, she and Michael would have gone to the mountain, but Carolyn, knowing only too well that she was avoiding facing the cabin again, decided at the last minute to attend a seminar in Eastern Studies being held on campus.

Her parents had written inviting Michael to spend a few weeks with them in Texas and he seemed anxious to go. Carolyn was glad because she had become quite worried about him.

At first he had talked about Mike constantly and had begun a new carving project using the tools Mike had left for him, being careful to give them the same care and respect as their previous owner. Carolyn had thought his project displayed the promise of talent, even allowing for the 'proud mother factor'. Of late, however the tools had remained untouched and he had stopped talking about Mike altogether. He had never acted this way before and Carolyn wasn't sure if it was growing pains or, as she suspected, the pain of not hearing from Mike.

In the first few days following Mike's departure he had perked up every time the 'phone rang and had eagerly awaited the mailman's daily arrival, but Mike might have dropped off the face of the earth, for they heard nothing of him. Nor was there any mention of him in the newspapers. Carolyn, to her shame, searched the business pages and the national gossip columnists daily for any tidbit she could find, but there was nothing.

She had never been able to sustain anger for any length of time and as it gradually fell away from her only pain was left. She missed Mike as she had not when she had first come from the mountain, possibly because then she had been in a state of numbed acceptance at his rejection. But now she had lain in his arms, had given him her body as well as her heart and soul. Each night her bed seemed emptier, her loneliness more acute but in the daylight his hateful words came back to wound, to caution. Carolyn misunderstood Michael's grief because it was her own.

There was no one to whom she could turn for advice. Even Steven was gone, acting as a guest lecturer at a university on the east coast. It was with relief that a spark of enthusiasm was ignited in Michael at going to see his grandparents in Texas.

He was curiously silent as she helped him pack for his trip. When she asked him if he was nervous at flying for the first time alone, he gave her a pitying look. 'Mom, this is the nineteen eighties. Lots of kids fly alone.'

Carolyn pretended to consider. 'Well, if you're sure. But I'll have them pack you a parachute if you're the least bit nervous.' He knew her attempt at humour for what it was and obligingly laughed, but Carolyn could tell it was half-hearted.

It wasn't until they were at the airport and he was getting ready to board that his worries came tumbling into the open. 'Mom, do you think he doesn't like me any more because I was sick?'

Carolyn didn't need to ask who 'he' was. 'Of course he still likes you, Michael! He wouldn't stop liking you because you were sick. After all, he was sick, too.'

'But I wrote three times and he never answered back. Not once!'

'You wrote to him? I didn't realise you had his address.' Carolyn's heart began thudding heavily in her breast.

'Well, it's his lawyer's address. He said he doesn't have a house anymore. He gave it to me when we left the mountain in case of emergency.'

'You know, honey, maybe he never received your letters.' Carolyn crossed her fingers behind her back and, in a sudden rush of guilt, added, 'Why don't you let me have the address and I'll give it a try. Maybe the lawyer didn't think it was important.'

Her son looked at her, doubt and hope warring in his young face. 'It's in my room, in my address book on the shelf over the desk. You will tell him where I am, won't you? Give him Gramma's address?'

'Yes, I will. Hurry now or they will leave without you. You're the last one on the plane.' He hurried to follow the retreating line of passengers after giving her a quick hug, his face bright and alive for the first time in weeks. 'Be sure and fasten your seat belt,' she called after him ... 'And 'phone when you get there!' He turned for a final wave at the door before disappearing inside and Carolyn felt suddenly bereft.

'First time?' came a voice at her side and she turned to see a small, neat greyhaired woman beside her. At her nod, the woman continued, 'It never gets any better. I've sent three of them off everywhere from summer camp to first jobs and I always think I should be going with them. I just put my youngest on board for Air Force basic training in San Antonio and I'm already lonesome.'

They continued to chat as they made their way to the parking lot and driving home Carolyn thought over their conversation. It was true. Time passed so quickly and before she knew it Michael, too, would be leaving for jobs, or the military, or college—or marriage.

But she wouldn't be totally alone. In a few months Michael would be having a little brother or sister. Carolyn had not been at all surprised when the doctor had confirmed her pregnancy. She had known that night that she and Mike had 'made a baby'. Nor was she upset about it. She wanted this baby and was thrilled at the thought of carrying it. If she could not have Mike she could have his child.

She wondered, though, how she was going to tell Michael and how he would feel after having her to himself all his life. And she wondered, too, at the ethics of not telling Mike. She wanted to put him under no moral obligations but at the same time recognised his right to know about the child. It was possible that with his low opinion of her, he would think the child someone else's when, and if, she told him.

Up until now the issue had been a moot point because she had no idea of where he was or how to contact him. Now she had an address and what she must do about telling him had now to be faced squarely for she had no excuse.

Also she must write to him in Michael's behalf. She had been relieved when she made the promise. In her heart of hearts she knew the love between the man and boy was deep and genuine. To cut them off from each other was something she had really no right to do. She had been wrong to try.

She had his address, or rather his lawyer's address. 'He said he doesn't have a house anymore.' How lonely Michael's childish words had sounded. No home. No loving family. And he loved someone else's wife. She mustn't forget that. Who was there for him when he dreamed in the night? Did he ever wake from his three o'clock in the morning battles missing her? Did someone else now share his sunrises.

Back at the apartment, she stared at the New Orleans address written in Michael's neat, boyish handwriting. New Orleans seemed a world away from the mountains of Colorado. She had decided that this time she would write only for Michael and see what the reaction would be, if any, before telling Mike of her pregnancy.

It was after many attempts and all afternoon that she had something she was willing to mail. In her letter she made no apologies for their quarrel but she did state her belief that she was wrong in not allowing him to see Michael. She told him of Michael's fear of the Sarge not liking him because he was sick. She gave him her parents' address in Texas after telling him not to let his feelings for her stand in the way of his relationship with Michael. Then she concluded with a hope for his good health before signing her name.

Afraid she might change her mind and start over again, she didn't reread the letter but folded it into an envelope and sealed it quickly. She addressed it, stamped it, and took it immediately to the post office.

That night, she slept fitfully, waking often. At one point she dreamed she was riding up the mountain going towards the cabin. Rounding a bend in the trail she came upon David sitting on a fallen log, Mike's carving of the wood duck in his hand. 'It's all right, Carolyn,' he said and flashed his familiar grin before waving her off. 'Hurry,' he called after her as she continued up the trail. She awakened with tears on her face.

Carolyn didn't look for an answer from Mike. She expected that he would contact Michael at her parents' address and that she would hear from her son whatever Mike had to say. When she received a fat legal envelope marked 'Special Delivery' with his lawyer's return address on it four days later, she was slightly stunned. She signed the delivery boy's receipt but stood turning the envelop over and over in her hands staring at its white blankness.

'Best way to know what's in it is to open it, lady,' the boy said cheekily. Carolyn didn't answer. She couldn't, but closed the door in his face without the least idea of what she was doing.

She carried the envelope into the kitchen with her and put it on the table as she poured herself a cup of coffee. Sitting down at the table she took a swallow of coffee before once more picking up the envelope and opening it quickly.

Inside was a note written in Mike's bold, unmistakable, almost illegible handwriting. It was attached to a legal document. She read the note first. It was tersely written:

Carolyn,

If anything happens, all I own is to go to you and Mikie. Attached is the deed to my half of the cabin. As David gave it to me, I give it back to you. If necessary contact my lawyer at this address. However, he knows how to get in touch with you if the need arises.

Mike

Carolyn's heart was knocking against her ribs and she rushed to the sink, suddenly violently sick. She washed her face under the kitchen tap and dried it before turning back to the table. She didn't have to pick the note up to read it again. It lay open on the table, the words written so boldly they seemed to leap into her brain.

Hands trembling, Carolyn picked up the deed and

scanned it. In five days time she would be sole owner of the cabin on the mountain.

What did he mean? Why was he doing this? The note sounded so ominous. Surely she was mistaking the meaning behind the words. She read the note again, still not touching it. 'If anything happens . . . As David gave it to me . . .'

No. Oh no. For a moment darkness seemed to swirl behind her eyes and she remembered Mike telling how much he hated being dependent on medication for the rest of his life. Had he stopped taking it and was expecting the worst. Or perhaps it wasn't working anymore. She recoiled at the implications. The note could mean anything—or nothing. She could be grossly over-reacting.

In five days time the cabin would be all hers. But why five days? Why not give her immediate ownership? Could it be that he wanted it for himself for that five days, that he was there now, perhaps making his own goodbyes. She remembered with horror the state he had been in the last time he had quit taking his medication. That time, too, he had sought solace on the mountain.

She looked at the clock, innocently ticking life away on her kitchen wall. Ten o'clock. If she hurried and didn't get a speeding ticket she could be at the Richardson's by one. That would put her at the cabin just about dark.

Five minutes later she was pulling out of the apartment parking area, headed for the mountains. She made good time but when she arrived at the Richardson's to collect her horse she found them very much against her going up the mountain so late in the afternoon. They wanted her to spend the night with them and leave in the morning, but Carolyn was determined. However, to allay their fears somewhat she

'Just a moment, boy,' Carolyn whispered as though the sound of her voice would conjure up her worst fears.

There in the grass by the stream, a dark mass in the reddish gloom. Carolyn looked and looked again. It was! She knew it was! 'Mike!' she screamed and started running, sobbing his name like a prayer. In the gathering darkness the mass moved and stood and started towards her. She stopped, unable to go another step.

'Carolyn?' Mike called. 'Carolyn!' But Carolyn didn't hear him. For the first time in her life she had fainted, sinking slowly and peacefully into the sweet meadow grasses.

When she came around she was lying on the couch in the cabin facing the fireplace. Mike was kneeling before it lighting a fire and as it caught, the flames illumined his strong face with its so kissable mouth. If it's a girl it will certainly be dangerous for her to have a mouth like her father's, Carolyn thought irrelevantly. Her eyes wandered over his face noting how pinched and tired he looked.

She must have made a small movement for he was at her side immediately, holding a glass of something fiery to her lips. She took a sip, knowing he would insist, though she felt no need of the stimulant.

'Hello,' he said and allowed her to push the glass away.

'Hello.'

He turned away from her to set the glass on the end table.

'How are you?' they asked simultaneously, and laughed a little together, each showing a trace of shy embarrassment unfamiliar to either of them.

'You first,' he told her. Seeing her movement to pull herself up, he helped her to a sitting position.

pointed out that she wouldn't be leading a packho
and would make better time than usual.

'I suppose she's right,' Mrs Richardson told
husband, becoming an unexpected ally. 'A pack ho
would slow her down and Mike has already taken
the supplies.'

He was there. She hadn't wanted to ask, afraid of
answer. But she couldn't hold back asking, 'Did he lo
all right?'

'Sure!' Mr Richardson grinned knowingly and th
frowned thoughtfully. 'Tired, mebbe.'

Tired—or sick? Carolyn swung into the saddle. The
Richardsons waved her off, not offering their usual
hospitality, knowing she would need as much daylight
as possible.

Carolyn took the trail up the mountain holding a
steady pace. She kept her mind fixed on journey's end,
giving her imagination no place in her thoughts. She was
frightened enough without letting her imagination run
riot.

Five hours later she emerged from the trees into the
clearing before the cabin. The sun was just settin
turning the sky into a glorious holocaust of colour
which Carolyn had no awareness. She slid from
horse, her legs barely able to support her, so tired
they from her long ride.

Leaning slightly against the horse, she surveye
clearing detail by detail. The cabin stood sile
door closed, no smoke coming from its c
though the evening was already cool as it be
quickly in the mountains once the sun was d
stable door, too, was closed. There wasn't a
anywhere. The stream tumbling over the ro
only sound except for a lonely cricket. He
and shook his head impatient for a much

'I'm fine,' she said. 'And you?'

'Fine.' He got up to add an unnecessary log to the fire.

'Why are you here?' He asked the question still in front of the fireplace, his back to her. His voice held no inflection.

'Because I wanted an explanation of that letter,' she said evenly.

'Oh? Didn't I make myself clear?' His voice was too bland, too emotionless and Carolyn had had enough. She had not raced up here for him to play games with her.

'No, you jolly well didn't make yourself clear!' she all but hissed, suddenly beside herself with fury. 'Would you leave the damn fire alone and turn around and explain yourself!' She was close to crying with an overwhelming rage.

He turned to face her then, still kneeling at the fireplace, a watchful look on his face, his eyes opaque but not hard. When he spoke his voice was flat and tired, the lines around his mouth pronounced. 'The letter was a sham,' he said. 'The words in it were all true. Everything I have will go to you if anything happens to me. I truly deeded my half of the cabin back to you. But I'm not expecting anything dire to happen to me in the near future. I wanted you to read more into it than was actually there.'

He paused. The only sound was the crackle of the fire and the lonely cricket, still chirruping somewhere. Carolyn's whisper could have been the sighing of the light evening breeze, 'Why?'

He turned his head slightly, to look once more into the flames. Carolyn had a clear view of his face in profile and the unhappiness in it twisted her heart. 'Because in your letter you said that you hoped that I was still feeling well. I took that very common, polite expression as a flimsy indication of some small bit of caring. I wanted to know if that were true and I picked this stupid way to find out.' His gaze never left the flames.

Her heart beating like a trip hammer, Carolyn's voice came clear and precise so that there could be no thought of doubt. 'Love doesn't turn itself off and on like a water tap, you know. Did you honestly think I would stop loving you just because I was angry? Justifiably angry, I might add.'

She was attempting a light tone, hoping to ease the lines etched in his face, but his face did not change and his answer was still grave. 'Yes, it was more than justified. And yes, I thought I had destroyed any love you might have for me. If I didn't, it wasn't from lack of trying.

'I thought I didn't want you to love me, that it was wrong and that you were betraying David. But when you said that about David's love being the giving kind and how he would have wanted you to be happy it suddenly came home to me how right you were and what an ass I had been. I wanted to apologise to you that night for all that I had said—and thought—but you were obviously in no mood for true confessions. I assumed that I had ruined everything and decided the best thing I could do was to get out of your life as you demanded. Then I received your letter a few days ago and it lit a spark of hope. I admit I was grabbing at straws.'

He continued matter-of-factly. 'I called Mikie, by the way, and straightened things out with him. Since I seem to have your blessing I'll be flying to Texas to see him in a few days.' Carolyn nodded dazedly.

He stood then, facing her but coming no closer. The only light in the cabin was firelight so that she couldn't see his face clearly. Mike's height put him out of range of its glow.

'I've loved you a long time, Carolyn—since even before David died.' His voice was heavy with self-disgust.

'But you didn't know me then,' she whispered, almost incapable of speech.

'Yes, I did. David talked of you constantly and I formed a picture of a warm, loving girl in my mind, a girl who could tackle a mountain and still remain joyous and feminine. You were the love of David's life, you and this mountain. When he first became my friend and talked about you, I wanted to meet and marry someone like you. But the more he talked, the more I envied him. Then you had Mikie and named him for me and I was ashamed of my envy. No one had ever paid me such an honour.

'David always shared some of the news in your letters with me and, God help me, I was as happy as he was when they came. It was as if you were *my* wife and Mikie was *my* kid. I worried about you being in the States alone with a new baby as much as David did.

'When he was captured and we eventually wound up in the same prison camp, it became worse. He told me all about you: the way firelight lights up your hair, the things that make you laugh and cry and angry.' He smiled slightly. 'Your ability to predict the weather. Never anything intimate, of course, but when he gave me that picture it was like he had given me you. The inscription on the back didn't have David's name on it, if you remember. Later, when I was transferred from one prison to another, I guess I went a little out of my mind. I would take out that picture of you and Mikie and it was *me* you had written those words to, you were waiting for *me* to come home. All the time I was hiding in the jungle, trying to get back, it was you and Mikie that I kept in front of me as my goal.

'One day, however, I found myself waking up in a hospital in the States and the first thing that hit me was that my best friend was dead and I had been having a mental affair with his wife even before he died. Suddenly I couldn't stand myself—or you, either. I got it into my head somehow that you were as much to blame as I. The irony of it was that I had never met you.

'It was a real laugh. I thought I hated you and yet I compared every woman I met to you and they were always lacking in some way. And, as you know, I've never been able to get rid of your picture.'

He continued talking, and Carolyn knew that it was as much for himself as it was for her. The sound of his voice as a catharsis for them both. At one point, she reached out silently and pulled him down to sit on the couch beside her. He sat, feet stretched out to the fire, head against the back of the sofa, hands as usual in his back pockets. He might have been relaxing after a strenuous day. They didn't touch, each knowing that now was not the time, yet his voice and her attention gave them a unity that exceeded physical closeness.

'I filled my life with work, and incidentally made a lot of money. People do when that's all they want from life. I filled my leisure with friends, associates, women. Yet every time I took a good, clear look around me, I seemed to have nothing worth having.

'Finally, a few months ago, I decided to break all my ties, get rid of all the things that bound me to a way of life that brought no satisfaction. As you know, I sold out—and in some cases, walked out of all my business interests. I sold my houses and apartments that never became homes, and went looking for something to give my life meaning. I went to Chicago to see my mother and brothers and sister. I had helped them all at one time or another and they couldn't understand why I had walked out on all that money and power.' He gave a small laugh of self-derision. 'I made them nervous. They thought I was crazy.'

Mike paused and rubbed a tired hand across his face before continuing. 'There was nothing for me in Chicago and I didn't know where else to go, so I decided to come here. I had been here a few times in the past and had never met you, so it didn't occur to me that you would be here at the same time. I drove across country and had plenty of time to think, maybe too much time. That was when I came to the conclusion that being tied to medication was as bad as being tied to making money. You know how smart that idea was.

'When I woke up in the snow with you bending over me, I thought I was hallucinating and wanted the dream to go on forever. I think I was a little disappointed when I found out you were real. Fantasies don't come true in reality. In your case, the reality was better than the fantasy. You were all David had said you were, but more, so very much more. And Mikie ... my god, he's a son any man would be proud to have. I found out then that you were why my life was so empty, that you were still my goal and my reason for staying alive. But in my mind you were still David's wife and I had cheated him once, in spirit if not in deed.' His voice was low and the self contempt in it wrung her heart.

'I wanted to hate you—tried to hate you, but you kept on being so damned lovable and giving. I thought in David's behalf I could hold Steven against you, and I did, even when I met him and found out what a really fine person he is. When you said you loved me I've never felt so good, nor hated myself so much for feeling that way. I believed that you had no more right to love me than I had to love you. I can only say how sorry I am for being so stupid.'

He gazed unseeingly into the fire as the flames snapped and hissed, the only sound in the quiet cabin for several minutes. They sat in the small world created by the fire's glow, surrounded by darkness and love and still he did not touch her.

'I'd walk through hell to hear those words again, Carolyn.' His voice was a low rumble that somehow conveyed months of tormented loneliness.

Carolyn reached out and touched the back of his hand that was now lying on the couch between them and he took her fingers into his broad palm. 'I love you more than life itself, Mike.' Her eyes searched his face, willing him to believe her. 'I have since I first saw you, lying in the snow, and I'll be loving you when I draw my last breath. There is nothing that you can do or say that will change that.' Her words carried absolutely conviction though they were spoken in little more than a whisper.

His eyes, in their turn, examined her face, but they were still haunted with a pain that tore at her. He ran a thumb over her cheek, his hand under the silken fall of her hair. 'You don't leave room for doubt, do you, lady?' he whispered. Gently he pulled her to him until her head rested under his chin. She could feel the warmth of his breath on her hair. 'Carolyn, I'm not sure I can allow myself to have you. I'm afraid that I will always feel like I betrayed David; that our life together would be a misery because of my guilt.' One big hand cradled her face against his heart. 'Do you understand?'

Against her will, she nodded miserably, listening to the dirge of his heartbeat. Two unhappy people held each other in an attempt to instill, one to the other, some small measure of comfort. But the warmth was only physical. Inside Carolyn felt the pervading chill of a terrible loss.

At last she raised her face and kissed him, but gently, on the cheek. 'Leave it for now,' she said and stood. They had both had all the emotion they could stand for the moment. Smiling down at him, she said brightly, 'I don't know about you, but I haven't eaten since breakfast and, as Michael says, I'm starving! What kind of supplies did you bring?'

Mike, too, stood up and headed towards the kitchen to light the lamps. 'The usual,' he answered. 'But Mrs Richardson sent a container of chicken soup. Isn't that supposed to be the sure cure for all that ails you?'

'Not only that, but right now it's the answer to a cook's prayer. Bless Mrs Richardson! I'm exhausted as well as being half-starved. And Mike, you look terrible! When did you last eat—or sleep?'

Mike was adjusting the cook stove as Carolyn poured the thick, rich soup into a pan to heat. 'Couple of days ago for both, I think. But don't worry, I'll leave enough for you. We can't have you fainting again from hunger.' He cocked his head at her. 'By the way, what caused you to faint the first time?'

'When I saw you lying in the grass I thought you were dead.' She kept her voice even, striving to keep the remembered fear out of it.

Mike looked at her a moment before saying gently, 'I was just getting a drink of water from the creek. I'm sorry.'

But Carolyn would not let the conversation turn serious again. They were both too tired. 'So you should be. I aged ten years and at my age I can't afford it. Now hand us down a couple of bowls.' She reached across him and removed the steaming pan from the stove.'

Later, too tired to make up the bed in the bedroom, she lay down on the couch fully clothed. She planned on sleeping on the couch but would rest a minute while Mike was washing up in the bathroom, before getting sheets and blankets for herself and changing into a nightgown.

Unexpectedly, she found herself awakening later in the night, the fire banked to glowing embers and herself tucked up cosy and warm under a comforter, Mike asleep in his sleeping bag between the couch and the fire. In the dim light, her eyes roamed lovingly over his sleeping face. The lines had smoothed out of it, giving him the look of being at peace. Carolyn hoped it wasn't an illusion. She closed her eyes again and in a moment her face was as peaceful as his.

When next she woke it was to the familiar tantalising smell of fresh-perked coffee. Her eyes opened slowly, to see Mike sitting on the floor beside the couch looking at her. 'Wake up, sleepyhead,' he smiled. 'It's almost dawn.'

But she seemed not to hear. A look of stunned surprise vocered her face for a long minute before it was completely illuminated with a radiant happiness. 'Oh, of course, of course!' she sighed, as though a great weight had been lifted. She threw the covers back and swung her feet to the floor, grinning from ear to ear. 'Oh, Mike, it *is* almost dawn!' she cried and hugged him. Before he could make a bewildered response she was on her way to the bathroom to wash.

Still fully clothed from the night before, it didn't take her but a moment to splash her face with exuberance and brush her teeth to the tune of an inner orchestra. Her shirt tail was hanging but she left it and went into the bedroom to find her moccasins. Over and over she sang to herself. That's it! That has to be it! Oh dear Lord, of course!

Carolyn's face was still glowing with suppressed happiness when she returned to the kitchen and when Mike looked at her quizzically she only grinned the wider. He handed her a steaming mug of coffee without comment and helped her with her jacket, for mornings are cold in the Rockies even in mid-summer.

Outside in the cool, invigorating air, Carolyn fairly danced. She twirled around and Mike caught her before she spilled her coffee, setting both of their mugs on the bench. 'I'm dying of curiosity, lady. What is going on?'

'Oh, Mike. I have to tell you. I was going to wait for the sun, but I can't!'

'Tell me what?' he smiled, indulgently.

Carolyn, now very serious, took both his hands in hers and looked into his face with fixed intent. For all her former exuberance her words now came slowly and she obviously chose them with care. 'It came to me this morning, just as I woke up. Suddenly all the things you had told me about David that didn't fit with the David I knew made perfect sense. Everything was as clear as if he had told me himself! Think about David, Mike.' As his face began to close she said impatiently, 'No, no. Not as my husband or as your friend! As he was as a man—as a person! Can you really believe that he was too blind that he didn't know your feelings for me? I'm telling you he *planned* it and knew exactly what he was doing. Don't you see?' she asked excitedly. 'David had many friends but he never had friends close enough that he would allow them into his personal life.

'But Mike, he allowed *you* in. He shared me with you, named his son for you. David knew, somehow, that he wouldn't be coming home. As you said, he loved me and this mountain. But there is a kind of love involved in friendship, also. As close as we were, whomever either of us loved, the other would love also. When David died he had taken care of everything and everyone he loved most in the world.

'I never believed that I could love someone as completely as I loved David—but David knew I would love you, because he did. And he gave Michael the only possible man that could take the place of his father. He gave you his share of the mountain, knowing you, too, would need a place of peace and beauty and knowing I would be here to share it with you. Mike, when he gave you that picture he willed you his family, knowing all the time you loved us as much as he did. He told you to tell me that it was all right, remember? He should have told you the same thing.'

She stopped speaking, searching his face for comprehension, for recognition of the truth in what she was saying. Her hands still gripping his, she pleaded softly, 'Don't deny or wrap in guilt that which has been given with so much love.'

Mike released himself to cup her shining face in his two large hands. That she believed implicitly in her own words was apparent. Could she believe enough for both of them? He looked into her face and heard a dead man's voice, sometimes strong, sometimes weak and faltering, filling his ears and heart and soul with a serene woman who lived on a mountain and waited for him—Mike—to come home. Gently, he drew this woman to him so that her head rested against his heart. The sun rose, unseen, in fiery splendour.

Later, when they could return to such mundane things as breakfast, Carolyn asked him, 'Where did you go when we left the mountain last time, Mike?'

'I went to see the old man who gave me my first set

of carving tools, those that I gave Mikie. I met him long ago, before I joined the service, and he thought I had talent then. I took him some of my pieces to see if he was still of the same opinion. He's blind now, and living in a rest home, but he can see more with his hands than most people with two good eyes.'

'Does he think you still have your talent?'

'Yes. Do you think you can be a wood carver's wife?'

'As long as the wood carver is you,' answered Carolyn placidly. 'We will live here, of course.' It was a statement and yet a question. At Mike's nod she smiled. 'Then the wood carver will have to be a carpenter first. We are going to need an addition.'

'I was thinking of that,' said Mike. 'Mikie needs his own room and I was wondering how you would feel about a generator, if for no other reason than to have enough electricity to run a washing machine?'

'Heavenly,' sighed Carolyn. 'There is going to be a considerable increase in the washing around here soon. I wouldn't think in terms of one room, if I were you. I'd think in terms of two.'

Mike looked at her in wonder and then pulled her into his arms. 'Oh, yes,' he whispered contentedly, rubbing his chin on the top of her head. 'When?'

'You have about six and a half months to get the rooms built,' she told him.

He chuckled softly, 'In that case, shall we start measuring?'

Harlequin Presents

Coming Next Month

879 THAI TRIANGLE Jayne Bauling
In Thailand an artist tries to bring two brothers together before it's too late. In love with one, she can't break her promise to the other—not even to avoid heartache.

880 PILLOW PORTRAITS Rosemary Carter
An assignment to ghostwrite a famous artist's autobiography seems like the chance of a lifetime—until he insists on her baring her soul, too, even her deepest secret.

881 DARK DREAM Daphne Clair
When her childhood sweetheart brings home a fiancée, a young woman finds herself marrying a widower who claims to love her. Yet he still dreams about his first wife!

882 POINT OF IMPACT Emma Darcy
On a ferry in Sydney Harbour it is a night to celebrate. Although the man she once loved is present, a model throws caution to the wind and announces her engagement. The shockwaves are immediate!

883 INJURED INNOCENT Penny Jordan
Co-guardians are at loggerheads—not so much over their differing views on how to raise the little girls as over an unresolved conflict from the past.

884 DANGER ZONE Madeleine Ker
An English fashion designer in New York is drawn to a successful merchant banker, despite his disturbing, reckless streak and the strain it places on their love.

885 SWEET AS MY REVENGE Susan Napier
The owner of an Australian secretarial agency is trapped and forced to face the consequences of her foolhardy act to save her brother's career. But no one tricks her into falling in love.

886 ICE INTO FIRE Lilian Peake
When her parents' marriage shatters, a young woman vows never to be burned by love. But at a Swiss chalet, a man who equally mistrusts emotion manages to melt her resolve.

Available in May wherever paperback books are sold, or through Harlequin Reader Service.

In the U.S.
P.O. Box 1397
Buffalo, N.Y.
14240-1397

In Canada
P.O. Box 2800, Postal Station A
5170 Yonge Street
Willowdale, Ontario M2N 6J3

Take 4 novels and a surprise gift FREE